THE WITCH'S SILVER LINING

WITCHES OF BEFANA BAY
BOOK ONE

DEANNA CHASE

ABOUT THIS BOOK

Welcome to the magical town of Befana Bay, located on the enchanted shores of the Hood Canal in the Pacific Northwest.

Sage Easton is a driven witch. At just thirty years old, she's an accomplished blown glass artist. Her glass creations are magical. Literally. But when a spell takes away her magic, suddenly Sage is unable to work and the only way to get it back is to learn to love life without her gift. Now she has to seek help from her old high school nemesis, the handsome and fun-loving man who has always gotten under her skin.

August West has one goal: enjoy life at all costs. He embraces the motto work to live, don't live to work. He spends his nights bartending and his days talking to orcas, photographing wildlife, and helping out whoever needs a hand. So when Sage Easton asks him to help her out, he takes it as his personal challenge to show the workaholic how to embrace the beauty of Befana Bay. But the tables are turned when the magic of

Befana Bay is threatened, and August is certain he knows exactly who's to blame. He needs Sage's help to track down the one responsible before life in Befana Bay is changed forever.

CHAPTER 1

"NICE MOON," August West called as he slowed to a stop beside the familiar red Toyota RAV4.

"Son of a—holy hell on a broomstick!" The shapely legs of Sage Easton kicked frantically from the open window as the petite blonde struggled to climb out of—or was it into—the vehicle.

August couldn't be sure. He wasn't even sure he cared. His lips were curled up into an amused smile as he stared at her bare butt cheeks and wondered what he'd done to deserve the glorious sight in front of him.

"Stop staring and help me, you perv," Sage ordered as she tried and failed to cover herself with the skirt that was caught on something in the cab of the SUV.

"Perv?" August shoved his hands into his pockets and rocked back onto his heels. "That's rich since you're the one mooning the entire town of Befana Bay. I'm just enjoying the show."

"I'm not mooning anyone," she said with a huff. "I'm wearing underwear, and my skirt is caught."

He raised an eyebrow, studying the backside in front of him. He supposed one could call the skimpy thong underwear, but it wasn't doing anything to hide the goods.

"August!" she yelled, snapping him out of his daze.

"Yeah?"

"Just take a picture if you're that fascinated. Then maybe you could help me. I'm late for the ball."

August momentarily considered whipping out his phone and doing exactly what she suggested but then quickly dismissed the idea with a shake of his head. He might be thoroughly enjoying this moment, but he wasn't a creeper. No, this memory would just have to live in his mind rent free for years to come.

He walked over to the driver's side of the vehicle and then peered in through the windshield, trying to determine the issue. "Do you know what your skirt is caught on?"

"I think it's the windshield wiper controls."

August scanned the dash and sure enough, the controller was sticking out of one of the holes intentionally embroidered on the outer skirt of her outfit. He couldn't help chuckling to himself as he moved behind her and then just stood there as he tried to decide the best course of action. "Were you climbing in or out?"

"Out," Sage said with a huff. "I got a flat tire."

"Is there a reason you didn't just open the door?"

"It's stuck," she said with a groan of frustration. "Are we going to play twenty questions, or are you actually going to help me out of my predicament?"

"I'm up for twenty questions if you are," he said, enjoying himself way more than he should be. Sage Easton was one of the most uptight people he'd ever known. Finding her like this, butt exposed in a ridiculous situation, was making him feel like Christmas had come nine months early.

"Don't be a jackass," she said quietly.

August sobered. He really was being a jackass, wasn't he? If he was chivalrous, he'd have already helped free her from the vehicle's window. To be fair, if there had been anyone else around to gawk at her, he wouldn't have hesitated. But he and Sage had a long-running history of needling each other. This situation had just been too good to pass up. He leaned against the SUV and tilted his head to the side, still trying to assess the situation. "Can I ask you a question?"

"Why not?" she said with a heavy dose of sarcasm. "Hanging out the window of my vehicle is the most fun I've had in months. You know what would make it better?"

He crossed his arms over his chest and shook his head, even though he knew she likely couldn't see the gesture from her position inside the driver's compartment. "Wine and candlelight?" he offered.

She snorted her amusement, making him swell with satisfaction. Nothing gave him more pleasure than smoothing the hardened edges of Sage Easton. It was the challenge he craved. He knew that about himself. It was why she'd always intrigued him. Of all the witches in Befana Bay that he'd asked out over the years, she'd been the only one to turn him down flat.

"Maybe another time. Right now, the only thing that could make this situation even better is if a news crew showed up," she said, letting her snark fly. "Now, ask me whatever you want to know so we can get on with this. My grandmother is probably already thinking of another curse to place on me since it looks like I'm flaking on her big night."

He cleared his throat. "Why didn't you just use your magic to get yourself free?"

"You're kidding, right?" she scoffed. "You were there when Gran stripped me of my magic, remember?"

August blinked at her. That had been... what? Three weeks ago? "Seriously? She hasn't restored it yet?"

"Obviously. Otherwise, I wouldn't be hanging here like a fool while you ogle my ass."

"I'm not ogling," he said with a laugh even as he let his gaze roam over her backside again.

"I can feel you staring right now."

Right. "Okay then. As soon as I get you free, we'll come up with a plan to show you how to have fun. Then the next time you're in this... *predicament*, you won't be stuck waiting for a handsome bystander to help you out."

"In your dreams, buddy. I don't need your help to have fun."

"I think that's debatable." He reached in the window and tried tugging at the skirt that was still stuck on the controls. But it wouldn't budge. He tugged harder.

"Wait!" Sage cried just as he heard the sound of fabric ripping.

Both of them froze and were silent for a long moment.

Then Sage let out a loud groan and slipped out of the SUV, her hands moving quickly to reposition the skirt so that she was completely covered.

August stared at the tattered skirt and grimaced. "Sorry about that."

Sage rolled her eyes before stalking over to the back tire. She crouched down to inspect the damage.

"Looks like you ran over a bolt," August said, noting the silver hardware stuck between the tread.

She closed her eyes as a muscle in her jaw twitched. No doubt she was beyond frustrated.

"Let's get your spare," he said, already moving to the back of the vehicle.

"I don't have one."

August paused and glanced back at her. "I'm sorry. Did you say you don't have a spare?"

She stood and turned to him, her shoulders back. "Yes. That's what I said. Why would I need one when I could just fix a flat with my magic?"

"That's a good question," he said, rubbing his hand over the back of his neck. He sometimes forgot how powerful the Easton witches were. August was a decent water witch, but his main magical skill was that he could communicate with animals. That particular skill had come in handy when he'd worked as a vet tech, but he'd eventually left that job because it was just too mentally draining. The local vet still called him in to consult on really difficult cases, but otherwise, August preferred his production assistant job in the film industry and doing odd jobs for the residents of Befana Bay. Sage however, had the power to manipulate things. Like broken doors and flat tires and making magical glass pieces that were infused with her powerful magic. His favorites were the everlasting glass lights that flickered with fire from within.

Sage cleared her throat. "August, do you think you can give me a ride to the ball?"

"The Witches Ball?" he asked, eyeing her from head to toe.

"Dammit, stop looking at me like that." She placed her hands on her hips and scowled at him.

"You're not going like that are you?" It wasn't just that her skirt was ripped. August eyed the formfitting T-shirt that she wore with the full black skirt and plain black flats. The outfit was fine for a regular gathering, but the Witches Ball? Everyone else would be dressed to the nines in corseted lace gowns, knee-high lace-up boots, and elaborate jewelry with every kind of crystal imaginable.

"What's wrong with this?" Sage glanced down at herself and grimaced when she spotted the ripped skirt. "Maybe I can get my sister to mend that before Gran sees it."

"I don't think fixing your skirt is going to do much to help this situation," he said.

"Stop being a jerk," she said as she walked over to the passenger door of his beat-up work truck that he used when doing odd jobs for the people of Befana Bay. "This is fine. My grandmother knows I'm not one for elaborate costumes. She's not expecting me to show up looking like Glinda from *The Wizard of Oz.*"

August couldn't help his snort of amusement. Did she really just say Glinda? "That's not exactly what I had in mind," he said as he climbed into his truck.

"What does that mean?" she asked as she scrambled into the passenger's seat.

"It means, Sage Easton, that I'm not letting you go to the ball looking like that. You might be late, but at least you'll be *fashionably* late in every sense of the word."

Sage blinked at him as her brow furrowed in confusion. "I don't understand. Are you taking me shopping or something?"

"Or something," he said, casting her a sly smile as he turned around and headed back to his house.

CHAPTER 2

SAGE SHOULD HAVE INSISTED that August take her straight to the ball. Sure, she looked a mess now that he'd ripped her skirt, and she'd managed to get a big streak of dirt on her T-shirt, but it wasn't anything that her sister Prim couldn't fix. While Sage was good at manipulating minerals, Prim's talent was with fibers. Her delicate magic would be able to repair the tear without anyone being the wiser. The dirt was another matter entirely. Maybe she could make use of the soap and water in the bathroom along with the hand dryer. Now that would be a sight to see.

August turned down a heavily wooded dirt driveway and came to a stop in front of one of the prettiest cottages in town. The blue house with the wraparound porch sat high above Befana Bay with one of the most spectacular water views in the county. How long had August been living there? Hadn't he been renting a small apartment downtown?

She turned to the man sitting next to her in the truck. "Isn't this Miss Penny's house?"

"It was," August said as he climbed out of the truck. "Are you coming?"

Faced with a choice of sitting in the truck by herself and waiting for him to take her to the ball looking like a homeless witch or following him into the house, she did the only sensible thing and stayed put. But after he disappeared through the front door, Sage couldn't help but feel petty. He was just trying to help, and she was being a petulant child. With a heavy sigh, Sage got out of the truck and headed to the front door.

"I was wondering how long it would take you to see the light." August gave her a cheeky smile and waved her in. "Follow me."

The inside of the house was just as charming as the outside. Eclectic artist-made furniture filled the living room, complete with what looked to be a handwoven rug covering the aged hardwood floors. August bounded up the wooden staircase, jerking his head for Sage to follow.

The stairs creaked under Sage's light footsteps, and for some reason she found herself feeling more comfortable in the small cottage then she did anywhere else except maybe her glass studio. Not even her grandmother's large Victorian right at the edge of the bay felt as welcoming and cozy as August's home. To say it was a little unsettling would be a massive understatement.

"This way, Sage," August said, opening a door at the end of the hall.

Trepidation filled Sage's gut as she stepped into what she assumed was August's bedroom. Why was he making her so uncomfortable? No, it wasn't that *he* was making her uncomfortable. August was being completely normal, welcoming even. This unease was coming entirely from Sage herself. And she didn't know why. She hated that she was feeling so awkward around him. She'd known August for years. And in all that time, she'd never really thought about him one way or another, other than having the impression he was just some guy in town who didn't have a lot of ambition. But he was nice enough, and even she could acknowledge that he was helpful. When someone needed assistance, he was the one they called, and he always showed up.

Helping her was all he was doing now, right? She needed to get over herself and just relax. They would only be there for a few minutes, and then they'd be back in the truck and headed to her grandmother's party.

"IF I REMEMBER CORRECTLY, there's a gown in here that's perfect for the Witches Ball," August said as he opened the folding doors of a large closet, revealing one side that was full of button-down shirts, flannels, jeans, and a couple jackets. The other side, however, was packed with colorful dresses.

"You keep gowns in your closet?" Sage asked, her eyebrows shooting to her hairline.

He chuckled. "Not usually. But it's good for you that I am now, right?"

Sage heard him but ignored his cocky smile. She was too busy gaping at the dresses. They were elegant and elaborate and looked like they belonged to someone who went to a lot of parties or maybe even events like award shows. That wasn't completely out of the question. Befana Bay was home to a lot of filming. August's first cousin, Leo West, had recently moved back to town and started a production company after acting for many years. A very popular television show had filmed several seasons in Befana Bay, and there were also the occasional movies. "Did you steal these from a set or something?"

August shook his head. "Seriously, Sage? You really think I'm just walking off with gowns that don't belong to me and then storing them in my closet until I find a damsel in distress who is in serious need of a stylist?"

"I'm not a damsel," she insisted.

"Sure, you're not," he said with a knowing nod. "But to answer your question, no. None of these gowns were taken from sets. If they were, I'd never get hired again."

Filming was one of the major economic drivers of the Pacific Northwest town. It was so important to the economy that the witches of Befana Bay had cast a spell over the small village so that paparazzi wasn't allowed anywhere within the town limits. Which made it even more attractive to A-list celebrities to both film and vacation there.

"Sorry. I was teasing. Mostly," Sage added with a smirk. "Whose dresses are these?"

"They belong to my roommate, Kelly." August flipped through the garments, searching as though he was looking for something in particular. After a moment, he pulled out a stunning turquoise corset dress trimmed with black lace and held it up in front of her.

"I can't wear that. It must have cost a fortune." Sage tentatively reached up and touched the satin of the bodice. Instantly she knew this gown was custom made by Beatrice Befana, a cousin of Sage's grandmother and a world-renowned designer. The fabric was just too luxurious to be made by anyone else.

"Of course you can," August said, giving Sage an easy smile. "Kelly won't mind."

"How do you know that? You can't just loan out someone else's clothes without asking them."

August just rolled his eyes and pulled out his phone. His fingers flew over the screen as he said, "Fine. I'll ask."

The phone dinged almost instantly with a reply. August gave Sage a self-satisfied smile as he held the phone out for her to read the message.

Sure. Someone should get some use out of it while I'm out doing shows. Enjoy the ball and tell Bethany hi for me. Miss you! At the end, Kelly had added two hearts and a kiss emoji.

"See?" August tucked his phone into his back pocket and held the dress up again. "Go on. Get changed. You're already late."

"Kelly's out doing shows?" Sage asked, feeling dumbfounded and a little shellshocked. Kelly wasn't just a roommate. That much was obvious. The two were sharing a closet, and Kelly had ended her message with hearts and kisses. The fact that August was dating someone shouldn't have been a problem. Sage didn't even really like him. Right?

So why did it bother Sage so much that August was in a relationship? He wasn't even her type. Was it just because she was having a bad day? Or maybe because she felt like a failure because she hadn't dated anybody in months? Hell, more like years if she was being technical. Sage had never measured her success by who she was dating or if she was in a relationship. Maybe she was just jealous.

The sinking feeling in her gut told her she definitely *was* jealous, but why now?

Goddess above, she thought to herself. *What in the hell am I going to do with that information?*

"I'll just leave you here so you can get changed," August said as he stood in the doorway, studying her for a long moment. Then he stepped out into the hall and quietly shut the door.

Sage clutched the gorgeous dress in her hands, still staring at the door. Then she shook herself out of her weird mood and glanced around, taking in August's space. There wasn't much furniture, just a queen-size bed and one dresser beneath the window that overlooked the bay. The bed was impeccably made with a crisp white duvet and bright purple and turquoise throw pillows. Likely that addition had been supplied by Kelly, Sage reasoned. The pillows seemed to be a touch too feminine for her to believe that August had purchased them himself. But what interested her the most was the unique art that lined the walls. As an artist herself, she was always drawn to original artwork.

Sage walked over to the piece that hung just above his bed and gazed at it with admiration. The artist had created a scene of downtown Befana Bay in a glass mosaic that depicted some of the village's most famous landmarks. She could just make out Brooms that Vroom, the shop that specialized in handmade magical brooms. To the left, the artist had added Tangled Up in a Spell, the yarn shop that had been there for nearly fifty years. And off in the distance at the end of town stood her grandmother's beautiful Victorian, where she watched over all of the witches of Befana Bay.

She wondered where he'd gotten the piece, knowing that if she had seen it first, she'd be the proud owner now. In addition to his mosaic, there were also a couple of paintings. One that was hanging on the wall next to the window was of the coven meeting at dawn on paddleboards with one of them talking to an orca. It was a beautiful acrylic with thick brush strokes that reminded her of DaVinci's style. The other one, leaning against the wall right next to the door, was even more interesting to her, as it was a portrait of Silas Ansell and Levi Kelley, the stars of a recent rock star romance movie. Why did August have a portrait of them? It was impeccably done, with the two actors gazing at each other while the background was painted in bright organic colors, making the subjects stand out.

There was a light knock on the door. "Sage?" August called through the door. "How's it going? Do you need any help?"

Son of a... She tore her gaze away from the artwork and stared at the door as if she were expecting him to walk right through it. When he didn't, she called, "Just need another minute."

"Let me know when you're ready for me to tie up those laces," August said, his voice slightly muffled.

"Right." Sage quickly stripped, and when she held up the dress, she realized there was no way she could finish getting dressed without his help. She stifled a groan and hurried to put on the gorgeous gown. When the bodice was covering her chest, she called, "Okay, I'm ready."

The door creaked open slowly before August poked his head in, deliberately keeping his gaze trained on the floor. "Are you decent?"

She let out a huff of amusement. "As decent as I'm going to get until we get this thing laced up."

August's head popped up as he walked into the room, grinning at her. "You're going to be the prettiest witch at the ball."

Sage rolled her eyes. "It's a dress, not a miracle."

"Miracle?" He raised one eyebrow and then scanned her body, his eyes finally coming up to meet hers. "I think your grandmother is right. You *have* been spending too much time in your studio."

"What does that mean?" Sage asked, craning her neck to look at him as he stepped behind her.

"You'll figure it out." He went to work, his fingers deftly tightening the strings of the corset.

Sage sucked in a sharp breath as the corset tightened around her waist.

August paused. "Are you all right?"

"Yeah," she said and then took in another deep breath, testing her comfort level. "It's all right. You just surprised me is all."

August tugged on the laces again, only this time as the corset tightened around her, she didn't feel as if her organs were being rearranged. "Sorry about that," he said. "Let me know if it's too tight, okay?"

"It's fine." She let out a soft chuckle. "I guess you can tell that I don't get dressed up that often."

"You should. This dress looks amazing on you."

Sage glanced up, catching a reflection of herself in the mirror mounted on the wall next to the closet. She fixed her gaze on August, noting he was staring appreciatively at her curves. A small tingle of anticipation rippled up her spine at his touch, and she froze, standing stock-still. Why was she suddenly attracted to August West? He wasn't her type. Not at all. Sage had always imagined herself settling down with a career-driven man. Someone who took his business as seriously as she took hers. This sudden fascination with August had to be just a fleeting moment. Maybe this was her sign that she needed to get out and date someone. Because if she was getting excited by the one man who irritated her the most, clearly it was time for a change. Especially since he was already involved with someone else.

"What's wrong, Sage?" August met her gaze in the mirror, his eyes piercing her with questions.

She cleared her throat. "There's nothing wrong. Why do you ask?"

"Well, your energy is screaming *don't touch me.*" He frowned as he studied her. "I'm wondering what I did wrong."

Oh hell, Sage thought. She needed to get her act together. "No, no. It's not you. I think I'm just nervous about borrowing your roommate's fancy dress," she lied. But it wasn't a complete lie, she reasoned with herself. She *was* just a little bit nervous about borrowing such a fancy dress. But that's not why she froze when he touched her. There was no denying that zap of electricity that crackled between them.

August finished tying her laces and then gently turned her around, his fingers lingering on her bare shoulders.

Her skin tingled beneath his touch, and she had a strong urge to lean into him. But she held herself still, trying desperately to keep from acting like a complete idiot. He wasn't coming on to her. All he was doing was helping her into a corset dress. *She* was the problem, not him.

"Relax, Sage. It's just a dress for your grandmother's ball. There's no reason to be nervous," August said. Neither of them said anything for a moment until something shifted in August's expression as he watched her. Then his lips curved into a whisper of a smile when he added, "Unless it's not really the dress that's making you nervous."

CHAPTER 3

August watched Sage in the mirror, completely amused. From the moment that he'd touched bare skin, her body had been filled with tension. He thought that it was just the unease of someone she wasn't very friendly with helping her get dressed. But when he noticed the gooseflesh on her skin, he knew it was something else entirely. The ego boost was like an adrenaline shot to his system. To know that he was affecting Sage Easton, that she was actually attracted to him? He'd never realized that she'd even looked at him in that way. And damned if he wasn't gonna have fun with this.

Sage let out a nervous chuckle as she placed her hands on her hips and tried to fix him with a flat stare. "I don't know what you're implying, August West, but if you're thinking that there's something going on here between us, then you're sorely mistaken."

"If you say so, Sage Easton," August quipped as he gave her a knowing smile.

"Oh, get over yourself," she said, waving a hand in his direction. "You're not the goddess's gift that everyone thinks you are." Her hand flew to her mouth as if she were trying to stifle the words.

August threw his head back and laughed. "So you been talking about me with your girlfriends, huh?" He felt his smile widen and wondered how long he could keep her in his bedroom. He quickly glanced at the bed behind her and couldn't help the dirty images that flashed through his mind. What would it be like to take his time undressing her, to run his hands all over her smooth, pale skin, to kiss every inch of her until she was pliant and ready to—

"Whatever you're thinking right now, forget it. It's never going to happen." Sage gave him a death glare.

"Are you sure about that?"

Shaking her head, Sage walked over to the door and grab the knob. Before she slipped into the hall, she turned back to look at him. "Let's just go before my grandmother starts thinking I was abducted on the side of the road."

"Wait." August reached for her hand, stopping her.

Sage stared down at his hand and then lifted her head up, her eyes piercing him. "Was this all just a ploy to get me in your bedroom?"

The fake outraged look on Sage's face made August shake his head. "Yes, Sage, you caught me. I'm the one who sabotaged your vehicle, caused you to get stranded on the side of the road, and then just happened to come upon you so that I could bring you back here to my bedroom. Then I decided to dress you up in a fancy gown just so I could take it off you again." Now that he'd said the words out loud, August half-wished that he *had* concocted such a plan. "You know what? Never mind. Just go wait downstairs. I'll be right behind you."

Sage blinked at him, her mouth open as if she were shocked by his words.

"Go on," he urged. "I'll just be one minute."

Sage reached down and grabbed the black ballet flats she'd kicked off before changing and then hurried down the stairs.

August quickly changed into a Victorian-style suit and then slipped into his roommate's room, opened the closet, and grabbed the boots he knew Kelly had purchased specifically to go with the gown he'd loaned Sage. Just as he was getting ready to head back downstairs, August's phone pinged with a new message.

Kelly: *Call me when you get home tonight. And be ready to give me every excruciating detail.*

August quickly tapped out a message: *It's not like that. But I wouldn't say no if she was willing.*

Kelly: *I have faith in you. I've yet to meet anyone who isn't susceptible to the August West charms. Now go make me proud.*

Chuckling to himself, August tucked his phone away and went downstairs to find Sage waiting for him by the door. He held the boots out to her. "These are for you."

She ignored the boots as she swept her gaze over him, looking him up and down in total surprise. Sage waved a hand at him. "What's this?"

He glanced down at himself, taking in the ruffled shirt and velvet jacket. "I couldn't exactly be your escort to the ball wearing jeans and a T-shirt, could I?"

"Uh, my escort?" she choked out.

He smoothed his jacket and gave her a cocky grin. "What better way to prove to your grandmother that you're learning to have some fun?"

"By taking you?" Her skepticism would have been irritating if he hadn't been enjoying needling her so much. "How does that prove anything?"

"I think your grandmother would be the first to say that I

both work hard and play hard. She's always told me she loves that I work to live instead of live to work. Admit it, Sage. I'm good PR for you while you work to get your grandmother to reinstate your magic."

Sage ran a frustrated hand through her long blond locks and blew out a breath. "Fine, but I can't wear those." Her gaze shifted to the hand-painted boots, and she actually looked pained as she turned down the offer.

"Yes, you can. Kelly bought them specifically to go with that dress." He nodded for her to take them off his hands. "Try them on at least."

"That's just taking this outfit too far," she said, glancing down at herself. "The ballet flats will be just fine. And then I won't have to worry about scuffing those or something worse."

"The boots make the outfit, Sage," he said, placing the footwear at her feet. "With those, you'll look like a proper witch instead of someone dressing up like one."

August could see it in her eyes when she relented. They lit up as she took one of the boots and admired the scrolling details. "Please tell me they didn't cost a fortune."

"They didn't cost a fortune," he lied. The truth was, everything in Kelly's closet was either designer or custom made. His roommate never skimped on fashion.

"Thanks for that, even if I don't believe you," she said and then stuffed her feet into the boots.

"Now you look like a witch fit for a ball." August held his arm out to her. "Ready, Miss Easton?"

"As ready as I'm going to be."

"Perfect. Your chariot awaits in the garage." His lips twitched with humor. "I figure it's best if we take my SUV so your dress doesn't get dirty in my truck."

"I definitely like that plan." She slipped her arm through his.

The moment her bare arm touched his, a spark of electricity tingled over his skin. His entire body suddenly felt alive. He paused for just a moment, surprised by his reaction to her. He'd always thought Sage was attractive, but he hadn't felt particularly drawn to her. He usually preferred women who were up for adventure. The ones who would jump at the chance to take a last-minute camping trip on the coast.

He was attracted to spontaneity. Women who had a zest for life. He'd always thought of Sage as responsible, steady, maybe even a little boring. Sure, she was an artist, and that interested him, but had he ever seen her doing anything other than working in her shop? The life she led was the polar opposite of the one he wanted to live.

So why was it that when he helped her into the passenger side of his SUV, he had a feeling that everything was about to change?

CHAPTER 4

"SAGE! There you are. Hurry up already. Grandmother is waiting." Lily grabbed Sage's arm and tugged her through the crowd toward the raised platform at the back of the ballroom. Floating candles were clustered overhead, looking like elaborate chandeliers, while champagne bottles were spelled to keep the glass flutes filled, eliminating the need for servers. Food magically appeared on the plates as hungry guests walked the buffet line, and the entire venue was filled with skin-tingling magic, making everyone feel like anything was possible.

The night was pure enchantment.

Or at least it was for everyone except Sage. She'd never really had that much fun at her grandmother's balls. She'd always felt slightly out of place, never dressing the part or staying long enough to participate in the celebration. If she had, there was a good chance she wouldn't be in her current predicament.

"Did she say anything?" Sage asked as she hurried behind

her sister, grimacing at the tongue lashing she was certain she was about to receive.

"She's asked about you at least half a dozen times," Lily said, glancing back at her older sister. Lily's eyes widened in disbelief, and she suddenly stopped, causing Sage to run into the back of her.

"Whoa," Sage said, raising both hands and catching her sister's arms to keep her from crashing to the old hardwood floors. "What did you stop for? I'm already in enough trouble."

"What are you wearing?" Lily's gaze scanned Sage from head to toe, the disbelief shining in her bright blue eyes.

Sage glanced down at herself, smoothing the gorgeous turquoise and black dress. "What's wrong? Did I already get it dirty, or did I rip it or something?" She ran her hands down the dress, frantically looking for any evidence that she'd already ruined it. "Please tell me I'm not going to have to buy August's roommate a new one."

"There's absolutely nothing wrong with it," Lily said. "It's freaking gorgeous. If there was a best-dressed contest at this ball, you'd be a shoe-in." Lily grabbed Sage's hands with both of hers as she stared at her sister in complete disbelief. "Did you say the dress belongs to August's roommate?"

"Yes." Sage's voice came out a weird squeak. She wasn't exactly prepared to talk about how August had not only rescued her but had dressed her, too. How pathetic was she?

"Okay, after you're done talking to Grandmother, you're going to have to tell me that story." Lily's face was lit with gleeful anticipation.

"There's nothing to tell," Sage started, not wanting to make this a big deal. "I got a flat tire, and August stopped to help me out. Then I ripped my skirt, so he took me back to his place and—"

"You went back to August's place?" Lily clasped her hands together and held them close to her chest, clearly desperate for the details. "Tonight, after this ball is over, we're definitely having girls' night. I'm going to need a play-by-play, right down to the moment when he asked to be your escort."

"He's not my escort," Sage insisted, just as August caught up to them and took her hand in his.

"You could have fooled me," Lily said with a smirk. She nodded to August. "Looking good, West. I like the suit. Very Dracula of you."

He gave Lily that sexy little half smile that was really starting to irritate Sage. "And you, Miss Easton, look like a fairy queen. Who's the lucky guy who gets to enter your magical garden tonight?"

Sage studied her sister for the first time, taking in the pale green dress that was embroidered with leaves and vines. She wore a delicate crown of twigs and flowers in her gorgeous blond hair. She really was lovely in every way.

Lily's lips curved into a slow smile, and then she threw her head back and laughed. When she got herself under control, she said, "You're naughty, and I like it."

He winked at her. "I like you, too. Save me a dance, will you?"

"You got it, handsome. Now go save my sister from our grandmother's wrath."

"I don't need saving," Sage insisted, suddenly irritated. Why did no one seem to think she could take care of herself? Never mind the fact that she'd needed August's help earlier. Those were extenuating circumstances. She could certainly handle explaining to her grandmother what had caused her tardiness.

"Of course you don't." August entwined his fingers with hers, and before she could protest, he pulled her to the raised platform and bent at the waist, bowing to her grandmother. "Good evening, Miss Bethany. You look ravishing, as always."

"August," Bethany said, her eyes sparkling. "I didn't know that my granddaughter invited you as her date." She turned her gaze on Sage and gave her a nod of approval.

"I didn't—" Sage started, but August quickly cut her off.

"She didn't tell you because she wanted me to be a surprise." August winked at Sage and then unleashed his flirty half smile on her grandmother.

Bethany let out a tinkling laugh. "You're such a charmer, August West. Make sure you spin me around the dance floor before the night's over, you hear?"

"I wouldn't dream of missing out on a dance with you," he said. "But first, I think I'd better get Sage out there before the men start lining up to try and take her off my hands."

"That's not going to happen," Sage muttered, suppressing the desire to roll her eyes. He was really laying it on thick.

Her grandmother eyed Sage from head to toe. "You look beautiful, Sage. I was starting to worry you weren't going to show up at all, but here you are, looking like a fairy princess." Her grandmother's tone was both light and loving, but Sage still winced. She hated that she'd been late. That she'd given her grandmother a reason to doubt her... again.

"It's my fault she was late," August said as he smoothed his jacket. "It takes time to look this pretty."

Bethany shook her head, but her smile widened.

Sage turned around, and this time she did roll her eyes, but she was smiling too. It was a little unnerving how easily August could win people over.

August grabbed her hand and pulled her onto the dance floor that was filled with the resident witches of Befana Bay and other guests. She spotted Levi Kelley and Silas Ansell, their heads bent together as they swayed to the music, both completely engrossed in each other. They wore matching tuxes with matching baroque vests. It warmed her heart to see the two men so comfortable in Befana Bay. After all the paparazzi that had harassed them over the years, she imagined they loved being in Befana Bay, away from prying eyes and invasive gossip articles.

Her sister Lily was dancing with Braxton Kirkwood, a new resident in town who'd just taken over the sporting goods store. He was a gorgeous man, six-two with black hair and bright blue eyes. In fact, he was so handsome that when he'd rolled into town a few months ago, everyone thought he was another actor there to film the latest holiday movie. When they'd all found out he was a regular guy, the single witches in town started casting their love spells.

Everyone except for the Easton sisters, that was.

Sage had three sisters. Lily, Prim, and Indigo. None of them would ever touch a love spell. Not after what had happened to their mother years ago. A shudder ran through Sage's body just thinking about it.

August clasped one hand to hers while wrapping the other around her waist to bring her in close to him. Then he leaned in and asked, "What's wrong, Sage?"

She pulled back and blinked at him, barely registering the fact that the happy, upbeat song that had just been playing had switched to the hauntingly beautiful song, "Mad World." Who was the DJ for this gig, anyway? Sage glanced around, looking for who was in charge, but when August pressed his palm to her cheek, she finally met his concerned gaze.

"What just happened?" he asked gently.

"Nothing. I—" She shook her head and cast her gaze to her feet. "Just a memory... of my mother."

"Oh." The word was filled with understanding. August pulled her into him, wrapping both arms around her and swaying gently to the haunting music. They were barely moving, making the dance more like one long hug.

Sage didn't mind. It was easy to bury her face into his shoulder, take in his clean, fresh rain scent and let his presence fill her senses. The connection went a long way to mask the pain she always felt when the memory of her mother's tragedy snuck into her mind.

She appreciated that August didn't say anything. That he didn't do anything other than hold her. Sage couldn't handle any of the platitudes or other well-intentioned niceties that people often felt the need to say when someone mentioned her mother's death.

When the song ended and a fast number came over the speakers, August pulled back then held one of her arms high before spinning her around and catching her. He quickly dipped her and stood her back up on her feet before she even realized what was happening. When August broke out into something that looked a lot like the jitterbug, Sage couldn't help the laughter that tumbled from her lips.

"Come on, Sage. Dance with me," he coaxed, keeping his gaze pinned on her.

Sage wasn't a dancer. And she certainly wasn't a joiner. But there was something magnetic about August that she couldn't resist. Before she could talk herself out of it, her feet started to mimic his movements, and together they danced through three full songs.

Finally, Sage came to a stop, clutching her side as she sucked in air. "I need a drink."

"So do I," August said, clutching her hand and pulling her off the dance floor.

Sage couldn't help but notice that all three of her sisters as well as half the attendees were watching them, their eyes wide with shock. She pressed her lips together into a thin line, knowing they were all staring at her. And why wouldn't they? Sage had never danced like that in her life. At least not in public.

"Ignore them, Sage," August said into her ear. "They're just wondering why their dates aren't twirling them around the dance floor."

"That's not at *all* what they are thinking, but I appreciate the effort." She accepted the bottle of water he held out to her.

He gave her a small smile. "Whatever they're thinking, underneath it all, they just wish they were having as much fun as we are."

Fun. Wasn't that why she was at the ball in the first place? To prove to her grandmother that she wasn't all work and no play? At least not tonight she wasn't. When Sage was done draining her water, she turned to August. "What else do you have planned for us tonight?"

He raised one eyebrow as his lips twitched.

"Get your mind out of the gutter," she said. But she held his gaze as her own lips curved into a smile. "Besides, I'm sure Kelly wouldn't appreciate you flirting with another woman."

He furrowed his brows. "Why would Kelly care who I flirt with?"

That comment brought Sage up short as she frowned at him. "Uh, half her clothes are in your closet. I guess I just assumed you two were dating."

His entire face lit up with amusement. "Me and Kel?" He chuckled. "Nope. Just friends. And those dresses are in my closet because Kelly has enough clothes to fill a small warehouse. I had some space. It's no big deal."

"Oh." Why did butterflies start fluttering in her gut? Nothing had changed. Just because August wasn't dating his roommate, that didn't mean she would entertain a relationship with him. Not that he was asking. Flirting didn't mean he was interested in anything other than having a good time.

His grin widened as he took her hand and said, "Come on. Let's show that grandmother of yours that you know how to let your hair down."

By the time the clock was about to strike midnight, Sage's feet were aching, but she didn't even care. She was exhilarated and felt better than she had in months. August had spun her around the dance floor more times than she could count. And even better, he'd given her his full attention, making her feel like she was the only witch at the ball. He'd done wonderful things for her ego. As much as she hated to admit it, she was starting to think that maybe her grandmother had been right. Making time for a little fun was exactly what she'd needed.

"Witchy Woman" by the Eagles came on over the sound system, indicating that it was time for all the women to gather and cast the blessing spell of the season.

August's hold tightened around her.

Sage looked up into his dancing eyes and knew he was just messing with her. "You know I have somewhere to be."

"What's wrong with giving your grandmother a little show first?" he asked, giving her a wink.

"You're going to give her the wrong idea," Sage said, shaking her head slightly.

"That *is* the idea." His gaze flicked to the raised platform very briefly before he gave her his full attention again. Then he bent and gave her a lingering kiss on her cheek.

Those tingles were back in full force, sparking wickedly

over her skin. The reaction surprised her, and she found herself leaning into the kiss even as he was pulling away.

"Whoa," he whispered as his hands tightened on her shoulders to keep her from stumbling forward. "Careful."

Sage stiffened and jerked back, her face heating in embarrassment. She chose to look past him instead of into his eyes. She just knew she wouldn't like the smug satisfaction she'd find there.

"Looks like it's not that hard to sweep you off your feet after all," he said softly.

She jerked her gaze back to his and rolled her eyes. "You just couldn't let that go, could you?"

"Would you have?" he asked with a tiny smirk.

No. She absolutely wouldn't have. But she kept her answer to herself. "Excuse me. They're waiting for me."

Sage hurried over to where all the witches had formed a circle. Her grandmother stood at the most northern point and indicated for Sage to take her spot between Prim and Lily. Indigo was on Prim's other side. The four Easton sisters clasped hands, and while normally their magic would spark to life as soon as they touched, this time nothing happened. Sage quickly let go of her sisters' hands and said, "Sorry. I'm the weak link."

"No, you aren't," Prim said almost defiantly as she grabbed Sage's hand again. "We can pick up the slack. It's what sisters are for."

Lily and Indigo followed Prim's lead. It took a moment, but Sage did feel a spark. Not one that came from her magic, but the one that came from the other three Easton sisters.

"She'll restore your magic soon," Lily whispered. "After tonight, how could she say you don't know how to have fun?"

Indigo cast Sage a skeptical glance just before she turned

her attention to their grandmother. Sage couldn't blame her. Their grandmother always walked to the beat of her own drum. While Sage wanted to believe she'd shown Bethany enough to get the curse lifted, she knew her grandmother would do whatever she felt was best, and she wouldn't be swayed by Sage's opinion.

Bethany walked into the middle of the circle with her arms raised high overhead. "Thank you all for being here tonight. As always, we'll pay our respects to those who came before us and bless the upcoming season. Please join me in manifesting a joyful and lovely spring that brings abundance in all forms to the people of Befana Bay."

Magic sparked in Sage's hands, zapping her fingertips. Joy burst in her chest. Her magic was back. Her grandmother had lifted the spell, and Sage felt freer and more relaxed than maybe ever in her life. Reluctantly, she silently thanked her grandmother for interfering. When would she learn that her grandmother only wanted the best for her? She vowed that the next time Bethany mentioned Sage working too many hours, she'd try to make some changes so she could enjoy the loveliness that Befana Bay had to offer.

But that joy fled the moment Sage raised her own arms and tried to join in the spell. Her magic sparked once and then quickly fizzled out, leaving her empty and without magic again.

Her entire body sagged with disappointment while all of her fellow witches reveled in the joy of blessing the season. Her grandmother, her three sisters, her cousins, and all of the witches she'd grown up with glowed with joyful magic.

Suddenly the combined magic came together in the middle of the circle and formed into the shape of a half moon and pentacle, the town's unofficial symbol. It floated effortlessly, and then when Bethany Befana called, "Let the coven's will be done," the magical symbol burst into tiny little fragments of light, delighting everyone in the hall.

A cheer rose up from all the guests before people started to say their goodbyes.

Sage waited for what seemed like half the town to bid her grandmother a goodnight, and once her sisters had hugged her goodbye, she made her way to the matriarch.

"There you are, Sage," her grandmother said, her voice full of happiness. "You looked wonderful out there on the dance floor with August. I do hope to see him around more often."

How was Sage supposed to answer that? She had no idea, so she didn't. Instead, she gave her grandmother a noncommittal shrug, hoping it conveyed a maybe instead of the *not a chance* that her mind was screaming at her. August had only been her date because he'd felt sorry for her. He wasn't going to be interested in afternoon tea with her grandmother's circle of witches or Thursday night cards when she and her sisters visited their grandmother once a week. "Gran," she started hesitantly.

"What is it, love?" Bethany asked absently as she checked the time on her delicate silver watch.

"I was hoping you could lift the spell that's suppressed my magic. I know you want me to learn some work-life balance, and trust me, I really am working on it. I came here looking like this, right?"

"And you cut up the dance floor for most of the night. It's not a bad start," Bethany said, nodding her approval.

"About that start..." Sage bit her bottom lip. "I really do need my magic back so that I can finish up some orders. I was hoping that since I've shown a willingness to try, that we could make a deal. I get my magic back, and in return I'll definitely make sure to take my days off and end each day at a reasonable hour so I'm not killing myself. I'm even thinking of taking up paddleboarding."

"Just one night of letting your hair down isn't what I had in mind. It's going to take a little more than that to convince me that you've really tried to learn to enjoy life outside of work."

"But my orders—"

"They can wait, Sage," she said disapprovingly. "Just tell your clients there's been a slight delay. They'll understand."

Instantly, Sage knew she had taken the wrong tact. She couldn't move her grandmother by complaining that her work wasn't getting done. Bethany Befana didn't care about any of that. She didn't need to. Money wasn't an issue for them. It never had been. Her grandmother operated under the premise that whatever good you put out into the world comes back to you threefold. Sage had to admit that she wasn't wrong.

Bethany was a kind witch who helped anyone who needed it, whether they knew it or not. And in return, she'd been blessed with an incredible amount of good luck. Her bank accounts were full, as was her heart. She likely only wanted the same for Sage.

But that didn't mean Sage appreciated her interference. At least not yet anyway. Sage sucked in a sharp breath and went for it. "What if I told you I was dating? And I started a garden and signed up for yoga?"

Her grandmother tilted her head to the side, looking past her and then meeting her gaze. "Is that true? Are you telling me you're dating August West?"

"Well, that's up for debate," Sage hedged.

"No, it isn't," August said, stepping up beside her and draping a casual arm around her shoulders. "We are dating. This is a date. And we have dinner plans on Friday night." He smiled down at Sage and gave her the tiniest hint of a wink. "And if I can talk her into it, there's a hike I'm planning Sunday morning."

Bethany beamed. "That's wonderful." She pursed her lips and narrowed her gaze at her granddaughter. "What did you plant in your garden?"

Sage cleared her throat. "Well, nothing yet. But I did order dahlia tubers and got seeds to start Zinnias. I also have big plans for a hydrangea section once I hit the nursery. I've already got a space cleared and have the materials for some raised beds."

"I'm going to help her build the raised beds," August chimed in.

"You are?" Sage asked, giving him a *what the hell are you doing* look.

"Yep." He nodded. "Tomorrow morning, actually."

"I have yoga in the morning," she said, remembering that she'd planned to be home early that night because her class was at eight o'clock.

"Cool. I'll get started and then we can knock them out once you get back." He gave her a conspiratorial grin.

Sage wondered why he was doing this. Why had he stepped in and assumed the role of helpful boyfriend? It was just all too much. She turned to her grandmother to come clean, to confess that they weren't dating and that she hadn't even so much as pulled a weed yet, even though she had *wanted* to start her garden. She just hadn't gotten around to it yet.

As soon as she opened her mouth to tell her grandmother the truth, the older woman placed a sure hand on Sage's shoulder and called out, "Restore!"

Magic crackled all over her skin, making every inch of her body tingle. As suddenly as the magic had appeared, it vanished, leaving Sage feeling lighter than she had in three weeks. It was as if a veil had been lifted and she was finally herself again. Magic tingled in her fingertips, and her entire body relaxed as she sighed in relief.

But as soon as she lifted her hands to admire the magic sparking on her fingertips, the magic vanished, leaving her feeling empty, like a void had filled her chest. She jerked her head up, her penetrating stare fixated on her grandmother. "What just happened?"

Bethany Befana shook her head slightly, looking a bit disappointed before she said, "I lifted the spell, but you weren't ready."

"What? Are you saying your neutralizing spell didn't work or that you revoked it?" Anger curled in Sage's belly, but she was careful to keep it in check. Yelling at the matriarch of the family, as well as the town, wouldn't gain her any favors.

"No, darling. I lifted the spell. All I ever wanted was to show you that there is more to enjoy in this life than work. I see you trying." She glanced at August, giving him a small, grateful smile.

"But my magic still isn't accessible. Can't you try again?" Sage asked.

Bethany slowly shook her head. "The spell is lifted. It's you who's holding yourself back."

"Why would I do that?" Sage didn't understand what was happening.

"That's for you to figure out," Bethany said. "Though I imagine once you're truly happy, your magic will come back full force."

Sage stared at her grandmother, her mouth hanging open.

"You'll figure it out," her grandmother said. "In the

meantime, I expect you both at my house for Sunday afternoon tarot." She glanced at August. "Four p.m. sharp."

"We'll be there," August said.

Sage wanted to argue, but all she could do was stand there and watch her grandmother walk away.

"That was intense," August said.

She turned to him slowly, her whole body numb with shock. Her vision blurred, and she blinked at him. When he came back into focus, she stared at his concerned expression and said, "I think I'm going to need a fun coach."

August let out a huff of laughter. "And you think I'm just the man for the job?"

"Yes," she said, trying but failing not to grimace. "Will you do it?"

He studied her for just a moment before his lips twitched into a small smile. There was amusement in his bright eyes when he said, "Hell, yes. Lessons start tomorrow at six a.m."

"Six! I have yoga at eight," she said, frowning at him.

"I know. Meet me at the marina. Trust me. You won't regret it." Then he nodded toward the door. "Let's go. You don't want to be late for your date tomorrow."

This time she did groan as she followed him out of the town hall.

CHAPTER 5

AUGUST WATCHED as Sage let herself into her small yellow cottage. Her home sat on the bluff on the north side of town, along with a dozen other original Befana Bay homes that were identical to hers, only each was painted a different color. They were the most coveted homes in town, facing the bay to the west, but rarely came up for sale. Most had been in their families for generations. The white one to the right of Sage's had been in his father's family until his grandmother sold it and moved to the blue house in the woods. The house he owned now. She'd liked her privacy. August couldn't blame her. He preferred the trees, too.

Sage turned in her doorway, gave him a pointed look, and then slammed her door shut. A second later, her porch light went out.

He chuckled to himself as he shook his head. Her message couldn't be clearer. Sage hadn't needed him to watch over her. But it was late, and even though crime was almost nonexistent in Befana Bay, he was still a gentleman.

August glanced at the clock in the dash and groaned. If he

was lucky, he'd get five hours of sleep before he was supposed to meet Sage at the marina. A yawn claimed his lips as he put the SUV in drive and headed toward his home in the woods. He knew the moment the house came into view that something was off.

Lights shone from the front windows. Lights he knew he'd turned off before leaving hours earlier. That alone was enough to alert him that someone was there. But the unfamiliar silver SUV in the driveway was a dead giveaway.

He frowned. Was it one of Kelly's friends? They did keep a hide-a-key under the large spider statue on the porch. He pulled out his phone and sent a quick text, but Kelly didn't respond. He muttered a curse, parked his SUV, and wondered if he should call the sheriff before entering his home.

The door swung open, and an all too familiar figure stepped out onto his porch and waved.

Son of a... What the hell was his father doing there? August climbed out of the vehicle and slammed the door, his good mood from his evening with Sage vanishing instantly as he met his father's gaze. "Most people call before they just show up."

Phillip West's easy smile vanished as he crossed his arms over his chest. "That's hardly the welcome home greeting I'd hoped for."

"This isn't your home," August shot back, climbing the steps of his porch. "Last I heard that was somewhere Back East with... What's her name? Stacy? Stephanie? Spacey?"

"You know damned well her name is Sissy. Stop being petulant. It's not a good look on you, August."

August ignored his father's reprimand as he swept past him into his home. He headed straight for the kitchen and grabbed a glass of water, despite his sudden craving for a shot of whiskey from his liquor cabinet. August rarely drank alcohol at home, and never as a way to cope. He was strictly a social drinker. But his father pushed all his buttons. It was his one true skill.

Phillip sighed, followed his son into the kitchen, and leaned against the counter. "I was hoping this visit would be better than the last one."

"There's a decent chance of that, considering the last time I saw you was when you were here for Grandma's funeral." August wanted to add that if anyone could make it worse, it was his father, but he kept that to himself.

"I know you're still upset about what went down at the lawyer's office, but can't we just move past that? I had your best interest at heart," Phillip said. As if he hadn't tried, and failed, to get his hands on August's inheritance. His grandmother, his father's mother, had left her house to August, not Phillip. The will had been ironclad, but Phillip had tried to get August to sign the house over to him anyway, claiming August could use the equity in the house to become a partner in his real estate investment company. In reality, he'd wanted to tear down the house and build another inn. He'd already met with contractors without August's knowledge. It was the straw that broke the camel's back in their relationship. "Besides, that was three years ago. Water under the bridge, right?"

August stared at his father, waiting for the contempt he'd felt that day to come rushing back. Instead, all he felt was numb. His grandmother had been one of the most important people in his life. And when she died, he'd been devastated. So devastated he hadn't even been able to step foot in her house. It had been too painful. Instead, he'd rented it to Miss Penny for the last few years. He'd only moved in a couple of months ago after she moved to Sante Fe to be with her grandbabies.

His father gave him an impatient look and pressed his lips together in a straight line.

August didn't have the energy for this. "It's late. I have to be up early. How long are you staying?"

"I was hoping to leave that open-ended. Does it matter? We haven't spent any meaningful time together in years. I have a break between projects and wanted to spend it here with you."

It took all of August's effort not to snap at his father. The audacity of showing up, unannounced, and expecting August to have all the time in the world for him was beyond irritating. His father always had been overly self-involved. He ground his teeth before answering. "Can we talk about this tomorrow? I'm beat."

"Sure, son." Phillip clapped him on the shoulder. "I hope you don't mind me using your couch."

What was August going to say? No? Then what? Tell him to get a room at the inn? Or better yet, go sleep at his cousin's house on the other side of town? Likely Leo and Nate's father, Michael West, would slam the door in his face. It's what August should have done, but his grandmother wouldn't have approved. *He's your father, August,* she'd always said with a kind smile. *He's not perfect, but he's the only one you've got.* For her, he buried his frustration and said, "No problem. There are extra blankets in the closet."

"Thanks."

August loaded the few dishes from his sink into the dishwasher and then disappeared upstairs. Once he was in his room, he leaned against the door and let out a long sigh. Why had his father shown up now? He'd left Befana Bay just a year after August's mother died, following Sissy to Salem. August had only been fifteen years old. His father left him with his grandmother, justifying it as not wanting to make his son move in the middle of high school. The truth was, August hadn't wanted to leave. But he hadn't wanted his father to leave him either. In the span of one year, he'd lost both parents. It was a wound that had never fully healed.

Thank the gods for both of his grandmothers. He'd lived with his paternal grandmother, but also spent a lot of time with his maternal grandma, Serena Simone. She lived south of town, deep in the woods, where she practiced her magic and took her involvement in the coven seriously. She was often Bethany Befana's right hand witch, except when she was away on one of her many trips with her bestie Camille. Like she was now.

"Stop," August muttered to himself. Going down memory lane wasn't going to solve anything. He crossed the room and disappeared into his bathroom to get ready for bed. By the time he slipped under the covers, he'd already put his father out of his mind and was reliving the evening dancing with Sage. There was a smile on his face as he drifted off to sleep.

A couple hours later, magic scratching at his skin jolted August awake, and he sat straight up in bed, his eyes frantically searching the room for his father. He'd know that magical signature anywhere. When he didn't see Phillip, he jumped out of bed and yanked the bedroom door open. But as soon as he walked into the hall, the intensity of the magic started to fade.

He frowned and moved back into his room, the clawing magic clinging to him again.

What had his father done? Anger coiled in his gut.

"Dad!" he called.

There was no response.

"Son of a—" A brilliant flash of white light shone through

his window. He didn't hesitate, and less than a minute later, he burst through the back door to find his father standing in front of a firepit, his arms stretched out to the sides.

"I welcome all the abundance this bay has to offer," Phillip called. "May the Befana Bay witches bestow their good fortune on my heart and soul." The bay just beyond the house turned bright silver, and when the wind picked up, it appeared to lift the magic from the bay and send it straight to Phillip. The silver light hit him right in the chest, sending him stumbling backward. He went down hard and landed with an *oomph*.

"Damned witches," his father spat out. "Always trying to keep a man down."

"Get up, Dad," August ordered.

His father whipped his head around. When he spotted August, he frowned. "What are you doing up? I thought you were beat."

"It might have had something to do with the amount of magic you were throwing around. Did you only come here to siphon the magic out of the bay? Typical." August shook his head and started to walk back toward the house.

"You'd be better off if you allowed me to siphon the magic of this bay for you, too," his father said, sounding unbothered by August's judgment. "Maybe then you could make something of yourself rather than being unemployed half the year. All it would take is a little bit of useful magic to turn your life around into something respectable."

August stopped midstep. His father had always been disappointed that August wasn't a more powerful witch. Sometimes it seemed as if he was embarrassed by his son. Maybe it was only fair, since August was embarrassed by his father.

"That's the difference between you and me," August said. "I

don't need to steal magic in order to find success in my life." He shook his head, unable to hide his disappointment. His father had never respected his work choices. The fact was, August could be employed full time if he wanted to be. There were a number of productions that would hire him as the lead production assistant. All it would take was a phone call, and he'd have a job tomorrow. He'd even been offered the production manager job on a few occasions, but he hadn't wanted that much stress. August worked when he needed to or when he wanted to. The rest of his time was spent enjoying life. And he wouldn't have it any other way. "I want you gone in the morning."

"You don't mean that," his father said with narrowed eyes.

"I do." August's words were firm. "You didn't come here for me. You came here for this." He waved a hand at the bay. "You got what you wanted. Now you can get back to Sissy sooner."

"That's not—" his father started.

"No. I don't want to hear it. Be gone by the time I get back tomorrow." Fuming, August stormed back into the house, bitterly regretting that he hadn't kicked his father out the moment he got home.

CHAPTER 6

SAGE STOOD at the water's edge and shook her head. "No. I'm not standing on a surfboard and paddling out into the bay. You do know how cold that water is, don't you?"

"You don't have to stand." August walked out into the water until he was knee-deep and then climbed onto his board and demonstrated sitting on his knees. "You can sit just like this and paddle around until you feel comfortable getting on your feet."

"That would be right about never," Sage told him, crossing her arms over her chest. "I thought you were my fun coach. This looks like pure torture to me."

"Can't you just trust me?" August asked. "Last night turned out pretty good, don't you think?"

Better than pretty good. Sage couldn't remember when she'd had as much fun as she had at the ball. There was no use denying that August was a major reason why she'd enjoyed herself so much. "That's different. If I missed a dance step, I wasn't going to be risking hypothermia."

August chuckled. "Okay, would you feel better if you sat on my board and I paddled us out a little?"

Sage wanted to say no. She even opened her mouth to shut his idea down. Instead, she found herself moving toward him and asking, "What happens if I fall off?"

"You won't. I haven't dumped anyone in the bay in over fifteen years. And even then, it only happened because that person cast a spell and ended up causing a disturbance in the water. And since you don't have magic…" He grinned at her.

"That was rude," she said without any heat and then moved toward him. "All right, Mr. *I've never dumped anyone into the bay*, tell me how to get on this piece of fiberglass without so much as dipping a toe into the water."

August dipped the paddle into the water and moved the board until it was parallel with the short dock. Then he hopped off the board and onto the dock and kneeled down to hold it steady with one hand. He waved her over. "Go ahead and kneel on it. I'll handle the rest."

Sage walked out onto the dock, just knowing that with her luck she was likely to be taking a dip in the water without ever leaving the launch area. But she was all in now, and her pride wouldn't let her walk away.

"You've got this." August held his free hand out to her.

She waved him off. "I've got it." But the moment she touched her foot to the board it wobbled, and she quickly placed her foot back onto the steady dock. She pressed hand to her heart, willing it to stop racing. "Uh, that didn't go well."

"It's better to kneel. Here. Let me show you." He placed one hand on the far side of the board and then the other on the near side. When he had the board held steady, he moved one knee and then the other until he was bracing himself on all fours. Sitting back, he looked up at her. "Your turn."

"How am I going to get on with you hogging the whole thing?" she asked, raising a skeptical eyebrow.

He rolled his eyes and then quickly stood without even so much as a bobble.

"You're insufferable. You do know it's annoying that you seem to be good at everything, right?"

"Insufferable?" He laughed. "Let's see how you feel after we paddle out. Now come on. Get on the board. You don't want to miss this."

She scanned the bay, trying to see what was so special. The sun was peeking out from behind a thick layer of clouds, the rays shining on the glassy surface. There was no denying it was beautiful. She just didn't know why she needed to be *on* the water in order to enjoy it. The view from the dock seemed to be just fine.

"Too chicken?" August taunted.

"Oh, hell no." Determined to prove him wrong, Sage followed his instructions and placed her hands on the board before climbing on so that she was kneeling in front of him. "There. Happy?"

"Yes," he said as he dipped the paddle into the water and guided them away from the dock.

"Whoa. I wasn't expecting us to take off so soon," Sage said, her hands gripping the sides of the board so tightly that her knuckles turned white.

"We're on a schedule. You have yoga at eight, remember?"

She grunted. "Yeah. It was the only open class."

"You'll need it after all the clutching you're doing. Relax, Sage. This is supposed to be enjoyable."

"I can't," she said, blowing out a long breath. "I just keep thinking I'm going to knock us both into the water. Then how am I going to get back on this thing?"

"No one is going over," he said. "Especially not with the escort we're about to get."

"Escort? What does that— Oh, sweet goddess," she said, awe in her tone as she spotted two orcas, one on each side of the paddleboard. The black and white creatures were magnificent, sleek, and powerful as they sluiced through the water. "You knew they'd show up?" she asked, glancing back at August, who was standing just behind her.

"They always do."

Sage expected panic to set in. The two huge beasts were just on either side of them. If one of them nudged the board or accidentally hit it, they were toast. But for some reason, all she felt was calm as the orcas dove and came back up, circling them.

August had stopped paddling, and they were idle in the water, watching the orcas carefully maneuver around them.

"What are they doing?" she asked.

"They're just saying hi."

They sat in silence, watching the orcas until one of them rose to the surface and shifted to her side. Her fin came out of the water, and Sage could've sworn the orca was waving at them.

"That's just incredible," she whispered. "Thank you for this."

"I didn't do anything but goad you into getting on the paddleboard," he said.

"Well, thank you for that. This is a morning I won't soon forget."

"Me neither," he said so softly she barely heard him.

Eventually the orcas moved on, leaving them alone in the bay. August paddled them around, and by the time they were headed back to the dock, Sage had decided she could stay out there all day long. The serenity was something she'd only ever experienced when she was in her shop. But there was something else out on the bay. A sense of rightness. Like all her troubles and concerns had vanished and all that mattered was that one particular moment in time.

"Do we have to go back?" Sage asked once the dock was in sight.

"No, we don't have to. But there's yoga and garden beds to build. If you decide those can wait, we can make another pass around the bay."

Sage was so tempted she almost blurted out that yoga could wait, except she'd already told her grandmother she'd signed up for the yoga classes. If she was a no-show, there was no way word wouldn't get back to Bethany Befana. And she didn't want her grandmother thinking she was a flake or that she'd lied. "As much as I don't want to go in yet, I think we'd better. I don't want to miss my class."

"You got it." August deftly got them parallel to the dock, and once Sage had her hands planted firmly on the edge of the wooden structure, she managed to get onto the dock with zero problems.

Sage knew she was beaming as she watched August maneuver the paddleboard toward the shore. She couldn't remember a time when she'd been so happy to be up before the crack of dawn.

Just before August started to climb off the paddleboard, a series of high-pitched sounds came from the water. He turned, tilting his head as he listened intently.

Sage wanted to ask him if that was an orca talking to him, but she instinctively knew not to interrupt.

The sounds got closer and without a word, August paddled back out away from the dock. When a large orca surfaced, he stopped paddling immediately and crouched down. The orca swam right up to him, made a few more sounds, and then was silent as he reached out and rubbed the whale's head. Its eyes closed as if the creature was reveling in his touch.

August whispered something to the whale, gave her one last head pat, and then stood on the paddleboard again. The whale stayed where it was, watching intently until August was back on the shore. Then it dove and disappeared.

Sage stared at him with her mouth open in complete awe. "Is that something that happens to you a lot?"

He shook his head. "They come visit me, but what the matriarch just did..." He swallowed hard, looking troubled. "She's never spoken to me like that before."

"She spoke to you?" Sage parroted.

He nodded. "It was a warning."

"A warning about what?" she asked, staring out at the bay, scanning the area to see if the orcas would return.

August turned to her and ran a hand through his thick, sandy-blond hair. "The magic of Befana Bay is waning, and if something isn't done, it could disappear forever."

CHAPTER 7

THE SUN BEAT down on August's bare back as he inserted screws into the planter box he was building for Sage. After their early morning trip on the paddleboard, she'd hurried off to yoga, and he'd made a stop at the local hardware store for supplies. In the forty minutes he'd been working, he'd already cut the wood for six planter boxes and had made good headway on putting them together.

It was amazing how much work he could get done when his mind was troubled. He paused to wipe the sweat from his brow and then pulled out his phone. Still no response from his father. Ever since the matriarch orca, Tokia, had issued the warning about the magic of Befana Bay, he couldn't shake the image of his father siphoning magic off the bay the night before. Did he have anything to do with the troubles the bay was having?

It wasn't the first time someone had stolen magic from the bay to bolster their own powers, but it worried August that the warning had come right after his father had cast the spell. In his gut, he just felt there was something off about his father arriving unexpectedly and then doing that spell in the dead of the night.

August had been out paddleboarding with the orcas every morning that week. It was his favorite way to start the day. If the trouble wasn't new, why hadn't they warned him already? Something had changed in the last twenty-four hours. And that meant his father was at the top of the list of people he needed to talk to.

He pulled his phone out of his pocket and hit his father's number for the third time in an hour. When it went unanswered, he shoved his phone back into his pocket and went back to work on the planter boxes.

He'd just finished the second box when he heard Sage's voice call to him from the back porch.

"Hey there, busy bee. If you keep that pace up, I'm going to have to keep you around for all my random projects."

He glanced up, feeling some of the tension ease off him. Sage looked adorable in her long yoga pants and a tank top with her hair piled high in a messy bun on the top of her head. Had he ever seen her looking so... relaxed? The way she was casually leaning against the support beam made her look like she was posing for an activewear ad. "I *do like* working with my hands. You have my number," he said with a quick wink. "Give me a call any time."

Her cheeks flushed, and she averted her gaze, appearing to be engrossed in the garden materials that were laid out just behind her porch. He loved that he'd flustered her, although he hadn't planned to be a flirt. But she'd started it with her comment about keeping him around. Pleasure wound through him, knowing that she wasn't as invincible to his charms as she pretended to be.

Sage made her way down the porch steps and came to

stand next to him. She reached out and touched his arm. "I can't stop thinking about that warning this morning."

He placed the power drill he'd been holding on the ground and ran a hand through his thick hair. "That makes two of us."

"I think we should tell my grandmother."

August had thought of that. In fact, he'd intended to head over to Bethany's house sooner rather than later, but he wanted to talk to his father first. He just wanted to find out if the problem was caused by his own father, and if so, whether they could reverse it without causing the head witches a lot of stress. Honestly, he also didn't want them associating him with a man who'd repeatedly used the bay's magic for personal gain. His father wasn't exactly revered in Befana Bay, but August doubted anyone knew the full extent of the shady behavior he'd exhibited over the years. August, on the other hand, was respected, and he wanted to keep it that way. If word got out about his father, no matter what August did, some people would consider him guilty by association.

"Yes," he agreed. "Bethany should definitely know." He pulled his phone out again, saw that his father still hadn't returned any of his calls or texts, and added, "You know what? Let me run a couple of errands, and then I'll swing by and pick you up so we can go see your grandmother."

"Oh. You need to go?" She lowered her gaze, scanning his body briefly before she blinked and looked away quickly.

August glanced down at his bare chest and bit back the self-satisfied grin trying to claim his lips. "Just for an hour or so."

"Right." She lifted her head. "Hey, if you're headed out, do you think you can drop me off at my RAV4? Prim stopped and fixed the tire for me this morning, so it's good to go now."

"Yeah, sure," he said with a nod as he walked over to grab

his shirt that was hanging off the porch railing. He pulled it on and then jerked his head. "Ready?"

"Uh... am I ready?" she asked, biting her bottom lip.

"To go get your SUV," he said, not bothering to hide his amusement.

"Right." Her cheeks flushed bright pink, but instead of averting her gaze again, she looked right at him and said, "You're dangerous without your shirt on. Do you know that?"

"Dangerous?" He chuckled. "How's that?"

"Oh, come on. You know you're hot. How could you not?" She arched one eyebrow. "Maybe warn a girl next time you plan to get all hot and sweaty and shirtless in her backyard."

"So you're saying I need to tell you if I'm planning to take my shirt off?"

"Yes." She placed her hands on her hips and gave him a pointed stare.

He could hardly believe this was the same woman he'd known most of his life. The one he'd thought wouldn't know a good time if it bit her in the backside. But here she was, flirting with him, and damned if he wasn't having a good time. "Got it. Any other rules?"

Her eyes twinkled as she smiled at him. "Not at the moment."

"Good." He held his hand out to her. "Let's go get your SUV."

He was sort of surprised when she actually slipped her hand into his. He held on, his grip firm as they walked around to the front of the house and his work truck parked at the curb. August opened the passenger side door for Sage. He waited for her to climb in and then shut the door for her.

Once he was in the driver's seat, she turned to him. "You don't have to open doors for me, you know. I'm capable."

"No doubt," he said, turning the engine over. "But there's nothing wrong with being chivalrous, is there?"

She shrugged. "I suppose not. I think I'm just not used to that."

He pulled away from the curb and headed toward town. "Who've you been dating, Sage? Pasty basement dwellers who wouldn't know how to treat a woman if they were given written instructions?"

"Do you really think I'd date a basement dweller?" she asked with a laugh.

He pursed his lips and shook his head. "No. I'd guess someone artsy. Or maybe a musician. But never an actor."

"Never an actor? Why?" she asked curiously.

"Most of them are too self-centered. You need someone who's more in touch with the world around them," he said.

Sage stared at him for a long moment. Then she nodded. "You're right. I do tend to go for the artistic type. Know anyone? It's been a while."

Me, he thought and then quickly banished the word from his mind. He was helping Sage, not trying to date her. Though the last twenty-four hours had convinced him that if he thought he had a chance, he'd definitely be asking her out. "I know some artists," he said then added a small white lie. "But none who are single."

She sighed. "The good ones never are."

What does that mean for me, he wondered. He was single. And an artist, though he doubted she knew that. Maybe one day he'd share that side of himself with her.

It didn't take long to get to Sage's SUV. August pulled in behind the vehicle and kept the truck running while he waited for Sage to inspect the tire and then climb into the driver's seat. He'd leave once she was on her way. But when she hadn't pulled away after a few minutes, he climbed out and went to her window. "Everything okay?"

"No," she said with a huff of frustration. "It won't start."

"Could be the battery. I have cables if you need a jump."

She shook her head. "I doubt it. It turns over but won't catch." Sage pressed the start button, demonstrating.

"Yeah, could be the alternator. Probably best to get it to the garage," he said, already pulling out his phone. He hit the number for Scotty, his friend who owned Auto Alchemy.

"What's up, brother?" Scotty asked after the first ring.

"Hey, man. Can you send a tow truck? Sage Easton's car is out of commission. Sounds like it might be the alternator."

"No problem." August gave him the location, and Scotty confirmed, "We can be there in about ten minutes."

August thanked him and then ended the call.

Sage raised both eyebrows. "What was that?"

"What was what?" he asked as he opened her door.

She let out a bark of laughter. "You're something else, you know that, August West? First you saved me from my roadside disaster yesterday, and then you saved me from a fashion disaster. And now you're taking care of me and my car again. Nobody is that nice."

"I'm not going to leave you here on the side of the road." August was confused. He hadn't done anything special. He'd just made a phone call.

"Of course, you aren't." She shook her head as she smiled to herself.

The tow truck arrived, and after getting Sage's information, the two men loaded it up and hauled it back to town.

August and Sage both climbed back into his truck, and Sage turned to him. "So, where are we headed?"

He pulled out onto the road. "Where do you want me to drop you off? Back at your house?"

"We don't need to go all the way back there. How about I just ride along with you to do your errands?" She gave him a bright smile, one he didn't see on her often. Or maybe never.

August stopped at a traffic light. "You want to go with me to run my errands?"

"Sure. Then we can go see my grandmother." When he didn't respond, she said, "Unless you don't want company."

August turned to look at her and saw the that her smile had vanished. He hated feeling responsible for the change in her mood. "No, that's not it at all. It's just that..." He ground his teeth together and then forced out, "I'm looking for my father. We're not exactly on great terms at the moment."

CHAPTER 8

THE SHIFT in August's mood the moment Sage had suggested she go with him to run his errands startled her. He'd instantly gone from his cheerful, helpful self to withdrawn and troubled. She'd never witnessed him when he wasn't the happy-go-lucky guy who was always willing to lend anyone a hand.

"Your father's in town?" she asked curiously. "Didn't he move Back East?"

"He showed up last night. I found him at my house when I got home from the ball." August's voice was flat, devoid of emotion.

"But he's not there now?"

He glanced at her briefly. "You know, I'm not sure."

"Why not? Did he have plans today?" Sage asked.

"I have no idea." August blew out a long breath. "I told him to be gone before I got back home today. The reunion didn't go well."

Sage winced and gave him a sympathetic look. "I'm sorry. It must be hard on your relationship being so far apart for so long. Do you want to talk about it?"

"It's only hard when he wants a relationship," August said, his eyes not leaving the road.

"That's rough," Sage said, feeling completely out of her depth. Her own father had passed away when she was just four years old. She only had a few vague but happy memories of him. She couldn't imagine what it would be like to have a father out there who'd just up and left when their child needed them most.

"Honestly, I don't think about him much," August said with a grimace as he pulled into the dirt driveway that led to his house. "Or at least I try not to."

"That's hard to do when he turns up at your house though," she said, sympathizing with him.

"And when you find him casting spells in your backyard." The house came into view and August parked his truck next to his SUV in the driveway. "His rental isn't here."

"The house appears to be quiet, too," Sage offered.

August undid his seatbelt and opened his door. "He's probably not here, but I better check."

"I'll go with you," Sage said, following his lead.

"This will only take a minute." August jogged up to the house, used his key to enter, and held the door for Sage.

Even when he was preoccupied with finding his dad, he was still holding doors open for her. Had she ever met a more courteous man? She really didn't think so.

August called out for his father, did a quick search, and then met her where she stood by his back door.

"What happened out there?" Sage asked, staring at a burned patch in the yard.

"Dammit," he muttered. "I didn't know his spell left a scorch mark." August rubbed the back of his neck and dropped his head forward, looking stressed.

"What spell was he doing?" Sage asked, knowing it wasn't something as simple as a blessing spell. It would take a lot of magic to scorch the earth.

A look of disgust flashed over August's face before he turned emotionless. But when he spoke, his words were laced with anger. "He siphoned magic out of the bay. It was so powerful it knocked him on his ass."

Realization dawned instantly. "That's why you want to find him. You think he has something to do with the magic waning in the bay."

"Don't you?" August asked.

She glanced at the burned lawn and nodded. "Yeah, that would be my first guess." She eyed the house and then the woods surrounding it. "He's definitely not here. Where else can we look for him?"

"My uncle Bruce's house. The inn maybe."

"Okay. I'm in. I've never met your uncle Bruce." She grinned. "I can't wait to ask him questions about young August and find out all your childhood secrets. Is he your dad's brother?"

"Yeah. One of them. He's the eccentric one who actually still talks to my dad. The other one, Michael, lives in the large two-story house right before the bridge that heads over to the Olympic Peninsula. He's Leo and Nate's dad. The two have been estranged since the day their mother died."

"Oh, family drama. Juicy." She rubbed her hands together, trying her best to make light of the situation for his sake. It was clear he didn't really want to talk about it.

August chuckled softly, and Sage could see some of the tension drain off him. "You know what?" he asked, eyeing her with interest.

"What?"

"I'm starting to think that just maybe your grandmother was too harsh on you. Neutralizing your magic so that you are forced to learn to have fun is really extreme. Especially since I think it was unnecessary. I just spent a big chunk of the past twenty-four hours with you, and I have to say that other than the arrival of my father, you've made that time thoroughly enjoyable." A slow smile spread over his handsome face.

"That was very nice of you to say. I really do appreciate it," she said, suddenly feeling shy.

His eyes flashed with mischief as he let out a small chuckle.

She narrowed her eyes, staring at him with suspicion. "What exactly are you thinking about right now?"

"Are you sure you really want to know?

"Yes," she said, giving him a pointed stare.

His expression was lighthearted when he teased, "I was remembering yesterday afternoon when I found you mooning everyone from the window of your SUV."

"Oh no, you didn't!" she shot back with a laugh as she moved to swat his arm playfully, but then she stumbled and fell right into his arms. His warmth enveloped her, and despite the fact that she felt like a total idiot, she couldn't deny that it wasn't a bad place to be.

August's arms tightened around her instinctively, catching her before she face-planted in the yard. "Whoa, easy there, slugger. You could hurt someone with all those limbs flailing."

"Ha, effing ha," she said dryly, trying to cover up the fact that she was enjoying this far too much. "I'm all right now. You can— Ouch! Son of a dirty jackhole!" she cried as she tried to take a step, intending to retreat from his embrace. Instantly she jerked her right foot up so that she wasn't putting any pressure on it while she clung to his arm.

"What happened?" August asked, scanning her foot. "Twisted ankle?"

"Twisted, broken. One or the other," she said, her voice shaky as the pain continued to radiate from her poor foot.

"It doesn't look like you can walk," August said. "Let me help you."

"Yeah, sure, okay— Oh!" Sage let out a gasp as August scooped her up in his arms. She wrapped her arms around his neck and leaned into his chest. He was so warm, so built. His chest was like a wall of steel. If she hadn't just injured herself and earned a trip to the healer like the flailing klutz she was proving herself to be, she would've liked to explore that glorious chest of his with both hands.

"You okay?" he asked, sounding concerned.

Sage swallowed and mentally scolded herself for perving over August. *He isn't your type, remember?* Even if he was, this was the worst possible time to be thinking about anything other than how to help him find his father. What was wrong with her? "Besides my ankle, yeah, I think I'm all right."

He gave her a quick nod. "Good. Let's get that ankle fixed up before it swells and it's too late for the healer to mend it with just one visit."

"I'm all for that," she said, biting back a wince when her foot jostled from his quick pace.

"Sorry," he said softly.

"It's not your fault."

He slowed and carefully maneuvered her through the house on their way back to the driveway. He bypassed the truck and put her down gently before he opened the backdoor to his SUV. "You need to keep that foot up. I figured you'd prefer the backseat to the bed of my truck." He gave her a quick wink. "Do you need help getting in?"

"I've got it." If she were a different person, she'd have said yes just to feel his hands on her body again. But she was Sage Easton, respectable witch and glassblower who was entirely capable of taking care of herself.

Right?

Absolutely.

There was no question she was capable. But climbing into the SUV with only one healthy foot would be a lot harder than just swallowing her pride and letting the man help her, right?

Sage turned to him and said, "I can do it, but it'd be easier if you just lifted me into the SUV."

"You got it." He immediately put his hands on her waist and gently lifted her up so that she was sitting on the seat. "Good?"

"Yep," she said a little breathlessly. "Very good."

August cleared his throat. He turned to avert his eyes, and if she wasn't mistaken, his cheeks were starting to flush pink.

A shot of intense satisfaction filled her. He was always the one disarming her. This time, it felt great to be the one flustering him.

"You're enjoying yourself, aren't you?" August asked when he turned to meet her eyes again.

"Yes, actually, I am."

They held each other's gazes, still smiling.

Then August leaned in and said, "Good. Just remember that when I finally get up the nerve to ask you out on a real date."

She blinked at him, not at all sure what to say.

He laughed. "Get your feet in the SUV so I can get you to the healer, Sage. We're wasting precious minutes."

"Right." She quickly scooted back, wishing fervently that she'd had some sort of cool or interesting comeback to his declaration, but she'd been caught completely off guard. Her phone buzzed with a text that made her groan when she read it. Her grandmother was bound and determined to make her life a living hell, wasn't she?

By the time August had gotten into the driver's seat, the text had made her forget she was shocked by his initial statement about asking her out. She leaned forward and said, "You better not wait too long to ask me out on that date. You wouldn't want to miss your chance."

"Are you saying I might have competition for your time, Miss. Easton?" he asked, glancing back over his shoulder.

"That's exactly what I'm saying, Mr. West." She held up her phone. "Check out the message from my grandmother just now."

August quickly scanned the phone. When he looked back at Sage, his eyebrows were so high they looked like they'd disappeared into his thick dark hair. "Your grandmother is signing you up to be a nude model for a six-week sculpting class?"

"Looks like it."

"And you're letting her?" he asked, sounding incredulous.

"Have you met my grandmother?" she asked with an exaggerated eyeroll. "There is no 'letting' with her. She does whatever she wants. I'm sure she thinks this will get me out of my comfort zone and would be something I'm interested in."

"Nude modeling is one of your interests?" he asked as he pressed his foot to the gas.

"No," she said with a nervous chuckle. "But sculpting is. I'd bet you a year's salary she did this just so I'd sign up for a future class at the pottery studio."

"But you're going to do it anyway? Model nude?" August asked.

She shrugged. "It's not something I'd volunteer for, but I

suppose I could try it. Maybe the spirit will see it as me letting my hair down and I'll get my magic back."

"I suppose that's one way of looking at it. Remind me to text your grandmother when we get to the healer's office and find out when that class is."

She frowned. "Why?"

He glanced back with a smirk. "Because I'm going to be their newest student."

CHAPTER 9

"You don't have to carry me," Sage said as August swept her up in his arms again. They were outside the holistic healing center at the end of the main road in town. Witch Tower Road was named after the Victorian where Bethany Befana lived now. It had a turret on the west side of the house that had been the lookout when Befana Bay had been a shipping town over three hundred years ago.

"I'm not going to let you walk on that ankle until we get it checked out," he said, kicking the door shut. "Not on my watch."

"You're kind of bossy, you know that?"

He glanced down at her pretty face, noted the tiniest smile on her lips, and decided that Sage Easton was definitely worth his time. Anyone who could handle a broken-down car followed by an ankle injury and still manage to smile was someone worth knowing. He returned her tiny smile and said, "Only when it comes to damsels in distress."

Sage rolled her eyes, but he heard the faint chuckle that

escaped her lips. She was enjoying him just as much as he was enjoying her.

At least he had someone to keep him in a good mood while he dealt with his father. The day could be worse.

Sage pulled the door open to the healing center and August carefully maneuvered her inside, making sure she didn't further injure her ankle.

The lobby was filled with eclectic overstuffed chairs in different styles and colors instead of hard plastic chairs like most clinics. It was one of the things he loved about their town. Everyone took pleasure in making their businesses unique and inviting. August placed Sage on an overstuffed red velvet chair and made his way to the intake desk.

"August," Cherry Callaway said with a bright smile. "What brings you and Sage Easton in today? Don't tell me you took her on that hike to the Devil's Cauldron. Sage probably hasn't seen the great outdoors since that time in second grade when her grandmother made us camp out in the backyard and that bat got in her tent." Cherry pressed her fingers to her lips to stifle a laugh. "I swear, you'd have thought a serial killer was after her with all the screaming. To think that a witch, even a young one, would be so terrified of bats."

"We were not hiking," August said, swallowing a sigh of exasperation.

"So just klutzy then? I'll get Mr. Kelley. I'm sure he'll be able to fix her up in no time."

"Mr. Kelley?" August asked. "What happened to Healer Jill?"

"She got called out of town on an emergency," a familiar voice said from behind him.

August turned to find the rock star, Levi Kelley, standing behind him. He was wearing ripped jeans and a black T-shirt with his Silver Scars band logo on it. "Levi? You're Mr. Kelley?"

"Last time I checked," he said with a smile as he walked over and gave August a one-armed hug. When he let him go, he looked August up and down and asked, "How's it going? Everything okay?"

"I'm doing all right, but Sage twisted her ankle about ten minutes ago. We were hoping the healer could take a look."

"Sure. No problem." He walked over to Sage. "Hey there. I'm—"

"I know who you are," she said, her eyes a little wide with surprise. "I think the entire town does. I just didn't expect to find you here."

He chuckled. "You're not the first one to say that. I'm a spirit witch with a strong talent for healing. In fact, before I took up music, I trained with a highly regarded healer and thought that was the path I was going to take. But it turned out it was too draining on me to do it full time."

"So how did you end up working here?" Sage asked. Then her eyes twinkled as she added, "Have times change so much that even rock stars need a side hustle?"

"Ha! No, I just enjoy the work, and since Silas and I are here for a while, I told Jill I'd be happy to cover for her if she needed a second pair of hands." He glanced at her foot. "Let's get you in the back so I can see what I can do for that ankle before the swelling gets too bad."

Sage started to push up onto one foot, but both Levi and August said, "Whoa."

She rolled her eyes and leaned back in the chair. "Well, what else am I supposed to do? Magic myself into the back?"

Levi called over his shoulder, "Cherry? Can you get us a wheelchair?"

August automatically stepped up and once again lifted Sage into his arms. "Don't worry about it. I've got her."

"So, here we are again," Sage said softly into his ear, making a shiver run up his spine.

He stared down at her but didn't say anything as he took in her wide-set blue eyes and the faint spray of freckles over her nose. He hadn't noticed them before and found them incredibly endearing. It made him think of their time out on the paddleboard that morning when the sun had started to shine down on them. One slightly wavy lock of her honey-blond hair was caught on her long eyelashes, and he had an intense urge to smooth it back.

Levi cleared his throat.

August jerked his attention to the rock star healer who was waiting for them by the door that led to the back. "Ready?" August asked Sage as if she'd been the one holding them up.

She just laughed, making all the tension in his body ease. "Ready when you are, Mr. Fun-For-Hire."

"Mr. Fun-For-Hire?" Levi asked as they passed through the door. "Is that a new service you're offering?"

"Only for me," Sage quipped. "He's determined to show me just how boring my life really is."

"That is simply not true," August said, defending himself. "I never said your life is boring. Seriously, Sage, you melt glass for a living. That's just downright fascinating."

She waved an impatient hand. "If you knew how repetitious it was, you wouldn't be talking about how exciting it is. Anyway, it's fine. I needed an injection of fun, and you're just the man for the job."

Levi sputtered with laughter.

August grinned at him while Sage's face turned bright red.

"That's not— Never mind," she said, shaking her head. "Can we stop talking about this now and just do something about my ankle?"

"Happy to," Levi said, still chuckling to himself as he led them to an exam room.

"Oh, stop it," Sage said, but she was smiling, too.

August set her on the exam table. Then he stood there, not exactly sure what to do. For any other friend he'd just take a seat and wait it out, but he wasn't sure if he should go back to the waiting room or—

"Sit down and stop hovering over me," Sage said. "You're making me nervous."

That settled it. He did as he was told and turned his attention to Levi.

The man he'd only known as a magnetic rock star and fledgling actor pressed the button to lift the table so that he could get a better look at her foot. He asked questions about the injury, how it happened, and if she'd heard a snap. Then he started probing to assess the damage. In those few minutes he'd completely shed the musician personality and turned into an utterly believable professional healer. August barely recognized him.

"You're a glassblower, huh?" Levi asked as he continued to probe the ankle. "You must be a magical one if your last name is Easton. You wouldn't own the shop on Witch Tower Road, would you?"

"I do," she said, visibly relaxing.

"Silas and I were in there the other day. Your work is incredible. I got a self-watering vase for my sister for her birthday."

"Thank you so much. I hope she loves it."

"I'm sure she will."

"So," Sage asked as she closed her eyes, grimacing when he ran his fingers over the area that was swelling already, "how long are you keeping this gig?"

"Just a few days while Jill is out of town. Then I'll go back to writing music while Silas works on his television show," Levi said.

"No touring plans yet?" August asked, wondering how they were going to work out their busy schedules.

"No, no plans in the near future. Silas will be filming the show here for the next six to nine months. I plan to be here for that. Seth and I are working on new music, and then we'll decide whether to launch a full-scale tour or just play select venues for a limited time. I'm kind of thinking we'll tour when Silas is on hiatus from filming. Then he can go with me. We both need some work-life balance. What that looks like, I don't really know, but we'll figure it out. For now, we're just taking it six months at a time."

"It sounds like you two are making it work," August said, knowing that they'd had problems before when they hadn't prioritized each other. They'd worked past that now and were both each other's biggest fans. August admired their relationship. They were two best friends who'd fallen in love, been torn apart, and then made their way back to each other. August hoped that someday he'd find himself a relationship as beautiful as theirs. His gaze landed on Sage, and something in his chest fluttered. Something he hadn't felt before. He unconsciously took a step back, uneasy with the new emotion.

"It feels like there's a tear in your ligament," Levi said. "But just a minor one. I should be able to heal it and have you back on both feet by tomorrow."

"Oh, good." Sage let out a sigh of relief as her entire body seemed to relax.

Levi wrapped his hands around Sage's ankle and closed his eyes. His lips moved, but no words came out as his body seemed to glow with a faint outline of magic. Without warning, magic sparked from his fingertips, and the light engulfed Sage's entire foot.

Sage let out a yelp of pain and jerked her foot out of his hands.

Levi threw his hands up in a surrender motion, his eyes wide with shock. "Sage, are you okay?"

"I don't know," Sage said, holding her ankle with both hands.

August moved to stand right next to her, protectively placing a hand on her shoulder. She glanced up at him quickly, her eyes wide, and then focused on her foot again.

"That's never happened to me before. I'm so sorry," Levi said, his voice shaking a little. "What happened? Did I injure you further?"

Sage started to wiggle her toes and then slowly rotated her foot. She let out a relieved breath. "It's okay. I think you might have even fixed it."

Levi reached for her foot but stopped himself just before he touched her. "Can I check it again? I just want to see what's changed. I won't be sending any healing magic to it again."

She hesitated for just a second before nodding. Then she reached for August's hand. He took it and held on, mentally sending as much positive energy as he could muster her way. Even though she appeared to be just fine, he knew that magic that goes astray during the healing process was very dangerous. Healing should only be done in the most controlled way, never leaving anything to chance. August trusted Levi and knew he'd never do anything to put anyone in danger. Whatever had just happened was highly unusual.

Levi pressed his hands to her ankle one more time, frowned in concentration, and then released her with a look of confusion on his face. "Well, the ligament has been healed. The magic worked. I just don't know why it hurt you. Like I said, I've never had that happen before."

Sage glanced at August. "It's probably because of the curse my grandmother put on me."

"Curse?" Levi's eyebrows shot up. "What?"

She sighed. "It's not really a curse. I'm just calling it that. She decided I needed to learn to have fun, and she neutralized my magic so I couldn't work all the time."

"That's not cool," Levi said, sitting down on a rolling stool.

August had thought the same thing when it had all gone down, but he understood that Bethany Befana had her reasons.

"She lifted the spell, but my magic has been twitchy ever since. Watch." Sage reached one hand out toward a jar of cotton balls on the counter. Magic shot from her fingertips and encased the glass jar, but then shot right back to her, zapping her fingers. She cursed and brought her hand to her chest, cradling it against herself.

"Sage!" August reached for her hand, but Levi was already there, prying her hand from her chest and inspecting it.

"Does it hurt?" the concerned rock star asked.

"No." She tested her fingers, bending all of them. "That was just a shock. I didn't expect it to spring back at me like that." Her eyes welled with tears, but she quickly turned away.

"What is it?" August asked, wanting to wrap her in his arms to soothe and protect her. The urge surprised him, and he found himself wondering once again what exactly was going on with him. Why was he acting like she was more than just a friendly acquaintance?

"Nothing." She shook her head.

But when both men kept staring at her with worried expressions, she threw her hands up. "What if this keeps happening? I'll never be able to blow glass again using my magic."

"That won't happen," August said automatically, knowing just how important her magic was for her business. "Your grandmother and the elder witches will figure this out. You know that."

"I really hope so," she said, angrily wiping at her eyes. "I'm sorry. I didn't mean to break down in the exam room."

"No need to apologize," Levi said gently. "I'm just sorry I hurt you."

"But you did fix me... I think."

"Why don't we see how you do if you walk on it?" Levi asked, holding a hand out to her. "Let's see if you need crutches or a cane."

She took his hand, placed her good foot on the ground, and then tentatively tried using her right foot.

August moved to stand right next to her, ready to catch her if her ankle gave out.

"Hey," Sage said, surprise in her tone as she put her full weight on her foot. "That's okay, I think." She let go of Levi's hand and took a step. Then another. And another. A smile claimed her lips as she beamed at the rock star. "You're incredible. Tell Silas he's a lucky, lucky man."

Levi chuckled. "Don't worry. I will." Then he glanced down at her foot. "Any residual pain or stiffness?"

Sage lifted her foot and moved it around in a circle. "No pain, but it is just a little bit stiff."

Levi nodded. "That's not unusual. If it starts to ache, take an anti-inflammatory. Otherwise, when you're sitting, write the alphabet with your toes. Do that three times a day until your full range of motion is back."

"Got it," she said and turned to August. "Ready?"

"For what?" he asked, furrowing his brow.

"To finish those errands." She held her hand out to him, and it was the most natural thing in the world for him to take it.

He slipped his fingers through hers and turned to Levi. "Thanks, man. I really appreciate it."

"I'm glad I could help." As Sage opened the exam room door, Levi glanced at their entwined hands and then back at August as he raised one eyebrow in question.

August gave him a one-armed shrug and a ghost of a smile before he turned and followed Sage out into the hall.

When they reached the front desk, August pulled his wallet out and handed over his credit card.

"What are you doing?" Sage asked, trying to reach for the card, no doubt intending to hand it back to him.

"I'm handling this. You fell at my house. It's my responsibility," he insisted.

She scowled at him. "It's not your fault I'm a klutz. You're not paying."

"I am." He thrust the credit card at Cherry, who was just watching them with an amused smile. "You're not going to change my mind, Sage. Just let this one go."

She crossed her arms over her chest and glared at him. "You're being overbearing."

"And you're being difficult. Are you always like this when someone is trying to take care of you?" he asked, aware that there was a challenge in his tone.

Sage rolled her eyes. "I don't need to be taken care of."

"Of course you don't. But isn't it *nice* to be taken care of sometimes?" He signed the credit card receipt and shoved his card back into his wallet.

"I don't know," she said with a frown as they walked out of

the clinic. "I guess since I moved out on my own, I'm just used to handling everything myself."

"When did you move out?" he asked.

"The day after I turned eighteen."

August stopped to give her his full attention. He was aware that she'd lost both of her parents when she was still young. After her mother passed, she and her sisters had moved in with Bethany Befana. "You left your grandmother's house at eighteen? Why?"

"I was sharing a room with my sister Prim, and privacy was nonexistent. Grandma's house is large, but two of the bedrooms are used as offices, and there never seemed to be a free bathroom. I don't know. I just needed space."

"Yeah, that would do it," August said. Her explanation was reasonable and valid, but he felt like she was holding back the real reason she'd moved out as soon as she could. There was a deep curiosity to know her better churning inside him. It was startling to realize he wanted to know all of her secrets.

"Are you okay?" she asked, frowning at him.

He blinked and then cleared his throat, still caught off guard by his realization that he wasn't just physically attracted to Sage Easton. He wanted more from her than just her body. So much more. "Yeah. Just thinking about where my dad could be," he lied. "Do you still want to come along to my uncle's or—"

"Yes. Let's do this." She walked over to the SUV and opened the passenger door. "Unless you don't want me to," she said hesitantly.

"Get in, Sage," he said, opening his own door. Now that he knew she was game to spend the day with him, he was all in. He just hoped she wasn't scared away by his crazy family.

CHAPTER 10

AUGUST TURNED the SUV down a tree-lined, dirt path. The road was rough as if it hadn't been maintained in several years, and Sage started to worry that they'd blow a tire.

They went over a particularly rough bump, and Sage gripped the handle near the roof to keep from bumping into the window. "That was enough to make my teeth rattle."

"Sorry about that." August slowed the SUV to a crawl. "I haven't been out here in quite a while."

Sage could see why. It wasn't exactly a quick trip. Uncle Bruce lived on the far edge of Befana Bay. Technically, his property wasn't in the city limits. It was on the outskirts in an unincorporated area. She guessed his address still read Befana Bay, but the home was thirty miles north of town. His nearest neighbor looked to be at least a mile away.

"You aren't close to your uncle?" she asked.

He shook his head. "He's always been a little… eccentric."

"What is he, a prepper or something?" she asked, glancing around as they parked in front of his house. There was an old school bus, a couple of boats that looked like they hadn't seen water in several years, and a beat-up railroad boxcar in front of the old two-story wood cabin.

"No, not really a prepper. Though he does live off grid. He's more of an inventor type. Always experimenting with some sort of magic mixed with technology. I think he fancies himself as a magical Doctor Emmett Brown."

"Doc from *Back to the Future?*" she asked, both intrigued and wary. If he was an inventor using magic, it made sense he'd be interested in figuring out ways to increase his power.

"Yeah," August said with a laugh. "He even has the white hair to complete the comparison."

"He's not into time travel, is he?" Sage pushed the door open but didn't climb out of the vehicle as she waited for him to answer.

August pursed his lips. "You know, I'm not sure. I guess it's always possible. But he's always been more into gadgets. Ones he can sell to normies that use magic instead of electricity."

Sage nodded. "Yeah, there's always going to be a market for that kind of thing." Though they existed, it was a rare witch who could infuse their magic permanently into something like a coffee maker or other small appliance. The magic just wore off too soon for the product to be worth anything. It's what made Sage's magic unique. When it was trapped in glass, it never faded. But if she tried to trap it in anything else, it just dissipated into the air.

"There is, except he hasn't figured out how to mass produce anything without burning himself out with all the magic he needs to expel. So he sells one-offs here and there to make ends meet."

Sage couldn't help it. Her thoughts flew out of her mouth before she could stop them. "It sounds like he'd really benefit from tapping the bay's magic."

"You'd think so, wouldn't you?" August asked. "But I'd be surprised if he's involved. He's very one-with-the-earth and always talking about not upsetting the natural order of nature. But if there is one person who can talk him into things, it's my dad. Let's hope he didn't get to Uncle Bruce." August jumped out of the SUV.

Once Sage joined him, August took her hand and led her up to the front door. Sage glanced down at their connection, wondering when they'd gotten so familiar with each other that holding hands had become the norm. Was it after all the dancing the night before or after he'd carried her all over town because she'd hurt her foot? She wasn't sure, but the one thing she knew was that she liked the warmth of his palm against hers.

August knocked on the door. When no one answered, he craned his neck to peer into the window. "I don't see anyone." He frowned and glanced at the driveway. I don't see his truck, but that doesn't mean he isn't here. With twenty-plus acres, he could have just driven it to the other side of the property."

"What now?" Sage glanced back at the SUV, wondering if they were about to go four-wheeling through the trees.

"This way." August tugged her toward the back of the house.

When they rounded the corner, Sage took in the stained clawfoot tub, the empty metal gardening tubs, and more terra cotta pots than anyone could ever possibly imagine. Random gardening tools were propped against the house, and bags upon bags of soil were piled up, indicating he was getting ready to start his spring garden.

"Looks like I'm not the only one who could use a hand when it comes to getting the garden started," Sage said.

August eyed the supplies and nodded. But he didn't say

anything as he led her past the backyard and down to the trees where there was a well-established dirt trail. It was just wide enough for them to walk side-by-side, but it certainly wouldn't accommodate a full-sized vehicle. The tall trees blocked out the sun, and Sage suddenly shivered from the dampness in the air.

"Wait," August said, throwing his arm out to keep her from moving forward.

Sage stopped suddenly and glanced around at the trees. "What is it?" she whispered softly.

"Do you feel that?" He crouched down and pressed his palm to the earth.

"Feel what?" Sage mimicked his movement and closed her eyes as her hand flattened against the ground. An electric shock zapped her fingertips, and she yelped as she pulled her hand away. "Never mind. I definitely felt that."

"The earth is steeped in magic," August said, standing.

"That's not really that unusual for a property that's been in a witch's family for many years, though," Sage said. Her own grandmother's house was full of magical surprises. "Is this a new development?"

"I think so." He ran a frustrated hand through his thick sandy-blond hair and blew out a breath. "Come on. We need to find Bruce."

They'd been walking on the same trail for a good ten minutes before it opened up into a clearing. To the right was a broken-down, rusted-out blue Ford truck that the vegetation was trying to reclaim. To the left there was an old white shed. The paint was peeling, and it was leaning to the right. Sage was certain that it would only take one good windstorm and the shed would be in shambles.

The door suddenly swung open and a white-haired man

wearing grungy coveralls appeared. His gaze landed on August and Sage immediately as if he'd felt their presence. Before he said a word, he stepped out and snapped his fingers, and the shed door slammed closed. The big padlock that had been lying nearby on the ground flew up and fastened itself to the rusty hardware bolted to the door.

"August?" Bruce asked with a deep frown. "What are you doing out here?"

"Looking for you."

The older man blinked in surprise. "Why?"

August kneeled and pressed his palm to the dirt. White light lit up around his fingers before it faded just as quickly. "When did this start?"

Bruce shoved his hands into his coverall pockets and rocked back on his heels. "Now that's an interesting question, isn't it?"

Sage studied August's uncle. The short, stocky man rubbed at his square jaw as he turned his expressive green eyes on his nephew. His shoulders were relaxed, and he had an easy smile. In contrast, August's brow was furrowed, and his green eyes were troubled. The two men looked nothing alike except for those deep green eyes. If not for that resemblance, she'd have had trouble believing they were related.

"Well?" August asked. "Are you going to fill me in or make me guess?"

Bruce chuckled softly. "You can if you want to, but we'll have to ask the powers that be if you're in the ballpark since I have no idea when the magic first showed up."

August's eyebrows shot to his hairline. "You don't?"

"That seems like something you'd notice right away," Sage said, knowing that she was subtly calling him out. The magic was strong enough that anyone with any power wouldn't be able to ignore it.

"Oh, I did. The moment I stepped out of my truck this morning, my feet started tingling. I tell you, I've never felt anything like it."

"You just noticed it today?" August asked. "So it happened sometime last night?"

"Oh, I don't know about that. I was down in Portland for six weeks. It happened sometime after I left and before I got back."

Sage met August's gaze and knew they were both suspecting the same thing. August's father had something to do with this.

August cleared his throat. "Have you heard from my dad recently?"

"Phillip?" Bruce asked, looking surprised. "No. Can't say that I have."

"He wasn't here when you got back this morning?" August pressed.

"Phillip's in town?" Bruce asked and then glanced around as if his brother would magically appear.

"He was. I don't know about now," August said. "He showed up last night and…" He shrugged. "We had words. It didn't go well."

Bruce nodded. "That happens. Phillip has always been a bit of a… challenge." He narrowed his eyes, and for the first time since they'd stumbled upon him, he wore a look of suspicion. "You think Phillip has something to do with this magic growing on my property?"

Sage cut her gaze to August, wondering what he would say.

"You know what, Uncle Bruce? I just really don't know. I

caught him siphoning magic from the bay last night. His spell knocked him on his ass, and now things just seem off."

The older man's expression turned stormy. "Phil was stealing magic from the bay?"

August nodded.

"That son of a—" He clamped his mouth shut and shook his head. "Selfish SOB. No wonder you had words. How can I help?"

August shrugged. "I'm not really sure other than to let me know if you see or hear from him. I think he messed up the natural order of things."

Bruce scowled. "He better not contact me. Not if he knows what's good for him." Then he pursed his lips together into a tight line. "Check with your cousin Leo. Phillip keeps in touch with him. Or at least tries to. He never could pass up an opportunity to social climb even off the backs of his own kin."

Leo West and his wife Priscilla Cain were fairly well-known actors who had moved back to Befana Bay recently so Leo could start his own production company. If Phillip West was the sort who used people for connections, Leo and his wife Priscilla would be prime targets.

"You're not wrong." August walked over and gave his uncle a hug.

The two embraced for a long moment before Bruce thumped him on the back and said, "Let me know if there's anything I can do."

"Be careful with the magic brewing on your property," August said. "As Sage said when we first noticed it, it's not unusual for the property of witches to develop its own magical signature, but until we know for sure what's happening, it's best to be cautious."

"I will, son." Bruce walked over and held his hand out to Sage. "It's Sage Easton, right?"

"Have we met before?" she asked as she slipped her hand into his.

"When you were—" A zap of electricity crackled between them, and Bruce yanked his hand out of hers as he jumped back, staring at her with his mouth hanging open.

"I'm so sorry," Sage started. "My magic is—"

"Tainted," he finished for her. He turned to August, his eyes flashing so dark they looked almost black. "The reason things seem off to you is because of this woman right here. Not your father." He turned back to Sage. "You need to leave my property immediately."

Sage opened her mouth to speak, but he cut her off as he pointed toward the trail.

"Go! Now!"

August stepped in front of her as if to shield her from his wrath. "Uncle Bruce—"

Bruce raised his arms in the air and started rapidly chanting a spell under his breath. Immediately the ground began to shake, nearly toppling Sage over. She met Bruce's determined stare, saw the steely look in his eyes, and reached for August.

"Come on. Let's get out of here," she said.

August hesitated for just a moment until magic rose up from the ground and started to snake its way around Sage's feet. Fear crawled up Sage's throat as she tried to take a step and found she was rooted to the ground. Her heart pounded against her ribcage as she opened her mouth to speak, but she found her words had been silenced.

"Stop!" August cried at his uncle. "Let her go and we'll leave immediately."

The magic vanished from Sage's feet, and when she let out a little cry of relief, she nearly cried tears of joy at the unintelligible sound she'd managed to make.

August wrapped his arm around her and steered her toward the woods. Just before they disappeared into the trees, he turned back to his uncle. "If you ever do something like that again, you're going to have to answer to me."

"Not if you're on my land," his uncle shot back. "Don't' bring her here again."

"Don't worry," Sage said under her breath. "I won't be back."

Once they were enveloped in the trees, August let out a shaky breath and said, "I'm so sorry, Sage. I've never seen him do anything like that before."

"It's not your fault," she said, hating that her voice sounded shaky. She was an Easton for crying out loud. Her family was powerful. The most powerful in the village. If someone came after her, there'd be hell to pay.

But that wasn't going to help her if she was thirty miles out of town dealing with a wacko who thought she was some sort of threat.

"It's my fault you were there in the first place." He rubbed a hand over the back of his neck.

"But you didn't know he'd react like that. You can't blame yourself for something your uncle did." She paused and then added, "Especially if his reaction has anything to do with the new magic bubbling beneath his property. Then it's neither of your faults." Sage knew well that foreign magic could do a number on a witch. Just look at her and how her magic hadn't come back even after her grandmother had lifted her spell. Magic was unpredictable at best. And downright dangerous at worst.

"No, but if my dad had anything to do with it, then I can't help but feel partially responsible. If I hadn't kicked him out—"

"Hey." She put a hand on his arm. "None of it is your fault, August. None of it." Her heart went out to him. How would she feel if someone in her family was responsible for attacking him? She'd definitely be taking some of the blame, even though in her head she knew she couldn't control what other people did. She sucked in a long cleansing breath. "Let's just go and find my grandmother. She needs to know what's been happening."

He nodded but was silent for the rest of their brisk walk.

Just as they reached the house, August said, "Wait a second."

Sage reluctantly paused beside him. The only thing she cared about at the moment was getting off Bruce West's cursed property. "What is it?"

He placed a finger to his lips and pointed toward the old bus that sat next to the boxcar.

She didn't see anything at first, but then her eyes widened when the medium-sized black bear strolled out from behind the vehicle. Sage instinctively moved to stand behind August.

Chuckling softly, he glanced back at her. "Leaving me to be the sacrificial lamb, are you?"

"You're the one who can talk to animals. I assume you'll just ask it to move on."

"That doesn't mean he'll listen."

Sage stiffened. She'd just always assumed that witches who could speak to animals had a special rapport with them. Was it possible they were about to be bear food?

The bear stopped, lifted his head, and then rose on his hind legs as he sniffed the air.

"Holy hell," Sage muttered, grasping the back of August's shirt.

"Relax, Sage," he whispered urgently. "He smells your fear."

"How am I supposed to relax when Yogi is about to eat my face off?"

"He won't eat your face off. I've got this," he said as he slowly moved toward the bear.

Sage was torn. She wanted to go with August but didn't want to be that close to the giant predator. On the other hand, if she kept standing where she was, she'd be left completely unprotected. It was as if her feet moved on their own as she followed him until they were right in front of the bear.

The creature turned his head and looked right at them before opening his jaws and letting out a loud roar.

Sage cowered behind August, praying to the goddess that he had some serious bear mojo skills. Because without her magic, there was nothing she could do to keep the thing from attacking.

August held his hands up in a surrender motion, and in a soothing tone, he said, "We mean no harm."

The bear suddenly snapped his jaws closed and stared at him curiously.

"We only want to talk for a moment," August added.

They did? As far as Sage was concerned, the only thing she was interested in was climbing back into the SUV and speeding out of there. If she never saw Bruce West's property again, it would be too soon.

The bear dropped down onto all fours and cocked his head to the side, waiting.

August kept his hands up as he let out a long slow breath. "I'm looking for some information on a man in his fifties. He's my height, a little thinner, but same coloring. He was driving a white SUV rental and thinks of himself as someone important. He has an air about him that reeks of superiority. His name is

Phillip West. I'm hoping you can tell me if you've seen him around here today. Or in the recent past."

The bear shook his head slowly from side to side and then made an unintelligible sound.

"Thank you. I appreciate it," August said with a nod.

The bear slowly sauntered off toward the old bus, only pausing once to glance back at them before disappearing into the trees.

Sage didn't waste any time. She sprinted to the SUV and climbed in, grateful to be safely inside of the vehicle.

August didn't share her urgency and was shaking his head as he climbed into the driver's side. "Did you really think the bear was coming back even after I talked to him?"

"Hey, I'm not taking any chances," she said, crossing her arms over her chest.

He chuckled. "Okay, fair enough. Do you want to know what he said?"

In her panic, she'd all but forgotten he'd asked the bear about his dad. "Of course I do."

"He hasn't been here. The bear said he'd know by the unfamiliar scent. No one out of the ordinary, other than you and me, has been out here in the last few weeks." August sat back in his seat and closed his eyes as he took a deep breath.

"That's good news, right?" Sage asked. "It means he didn't have anything to do with the magic here."

"Right. But we still don't know where he went."

Sage reached over and placed her hand over his as she said, "Let's just go find my grandmother. I think it's time to let the coven know what's going on."

"Yeah, okay," August said, sounding defeated. "I just wish I'd found my father first."

"You're not responsible for his actions, August. You know that, right?"

He nodded. "I do. I just can't help feeling like I could have done something."

She squeezed his hand. "I know, August. I know."

CHAPTER 11

"ARE YOU SURE SHE'S HERE?" August asked Sage when she knocked on Bethany's door for the third time.

"I don't know where else she would be. It's Sunday. Usually, she has a coven meeting in the morning and then afternoon tea at four. Right about now she should be making the cookies she plans to serve." Sage frowned and then jerked her head, indicating he should follow her.

The two of them walked along the wraparound porch until they reached the back of the house. There was a wooden swing hanging from the porch roof as well as twinkle lights covering nearly every inch of the back porch area. It must have been something incredible when the lights were lit.

The back door swung open, and Bethany startled when she spotted them. "Sage? August? What are you doing here? We didn't have plans today, did we?"

"No," Sage said. She looked her grandmother up and down and then frowned. "What's wrong?"

Bethany waved an impatient hand. "It's coven business. Nothing you need to worry about."

August cleared his throat. "I'm sorry to bother you, Bethany, but there's something we think you need to know."

"I'm sorry, August. It's going to have to wait," she said impatiently. "I have a meeting to get to and I can't be late." She reached up and grabbed a crystal that was hanging over the wooden swing and then slipped back into the house.

Sage pulled the door open and gestured for August to join her. He hesitated, but when she strode into the house, his feet propelled him forward and he slipped in behind her. The warm inviting magic that lived in the Befana house enveloped him, making him feel as if everything was right in the world. The difference between the Befana home magic and the magic infused on his uncle's property was like night and day. This magic made him feel connected to the earth and everything around as if he belonged. His uncle's had mildly irritated him from the inside out.

"Grandma?" Sage called from the doorway of the kitchen that led into a sitting room.

The older woman appeared from what looked to be the formal dining room. "Sage, I told you—"

"August got a message from the matriarch orca that the magic in the bay is dying," she blurted.

Bethany just nodded. "Yes, dear. I'm aware. That's what I have to go take care of. No time to talk." Then she looked at August. "Thank you for coming to me, but I have to go now." The older witch disappeared, and a few seconds later, they heard the front door slam.

August leaned against one of the counters and let out a long breath. "Well, I guess that's it then."

"How do you think she knew?" Sage asked. "It's not like talking to orcas is a widespread skill."

"That's a really good question, but I suppose a water witch

may have noticed something strange," he reasoned and then decided he was just going to put the entire thing out of his mind. He'd spent the whole day worrying and chasing his father, when what he really should have done was just go straight to Bethany Befana. He'd been stupid to think that no one else would have noticed the problem with the bay.

"So…" Sage started. "Can I buy you a late lunch as a thank you for helping me with my garden?"

"You don't owe me anything," he said, pushing off the counter. "That was just a favor for a friend."

"So you can do a favor for me, but I can't do one for you?" she asked, her eyebrows raised.

Well damn, when she put it like that, he couldn't just brush her off. "The Salt Circle?" he asked, referring to the town pub.

She grinned. "Perfect." Sage waved a hand, indicating that he should follow her and then led him out the front door.

They walked the few short blocks to the pub that sat overlooking the bay and were seated outside under a covered patio.

August was so familiar with the menu he didn't even need to look at it.

Before they could even speak, Gavin, the pub owner's grandson, was there, pulling up a chair beside Sage. The Salt Circle was a family run operation, as the pub had been in the family for over a hundred years. "Hey, you two. Long time no see."

Gavin was a good friend of August's, but he'd been out of town for a while, working at his cousin's pub in Salem to help them out after their father had died suddenly in a freak accident. "You're back. How was Salem?"

"Cold," he said with a chuckle. "But The Black Cauldron is fully staffed and back at full speed, so that's good."

Sage reached over and squeezed his hand. "I'm sorry for your loss. It was good of you to go out there and help."

He smiled at her. "It's what family does, right?"

"Absolutely," Sage said as she went on to talk about how her entire family helped their aunt out with her clothing business that one time when she'd been sick with Witch's Flu. It was a virus that affected only witches and often hung around for months.

August sat back, suddenly wondering who in his family would show up for him if he needed them. Certainly not his father. Maybe his cousins, though they weren't really that close. Plus, both Leo and Nate were busy with their own demanding careers. He had friends of course. Levi and Silas, Gavin, and plenty of residents of Befana Bay. However, there were only two people August truly thought he could count on no matter what. One was his roommate Kelly. They were ride or die. The second was his grandmother Serena. She'd lay down her life for him if need be and vice versa. But she'd entered her golden years and was living her best life traveling the world most of the time. It's what he wanted for her. Not for her to be hanging around Befana Bay, keeping an eye out just in case he needed her one day.

What would it be like to have a close-knit family one could fall back on with no questions asked? August had no idea.

Gavin placed a hand on August's shoulder. "What can I get you to drink?"

"I'll have The Salt Circle Lager," August said.

"And I'll have the Blue Mist," Sage said, referring to the pub's wheat beer.

"You got it." He glanced at Sage and then gave August a quick questioning glance, no doubt wondering what was happening between them.

August gave him a tiny shake of his head. Gavin nodded once and disappeared back into the pub.

"What was that about?" Sage asked, her lips curving into a hint of a smile.

August chuckled. "He wants to know if we're dating."

"And you told him no?" she asked with her eyebrows raised.

"I didn't exactly tell him no. I sort of brushed him off." August leaned forward, giving her his amused half smile. "Are you saying you want to go public?"

Her cheeks turned pink, and August's chest swelled with triumph. Gods, he loved getting under her skin. She cleared her throat. "It's not that I want to make a spectacle of things, but we did tell my grandmother that we're dating. If we don't want her to know that we lied, then—"

"We need to go all in on this," he finished for her, leaning back and nodding. "I'm in if you are."

She hesitated, and for a second he thought she was going to back out. But then she shrugged and gave him a shy smile. "I guess I'm in."

When Gavin reappeared with their drinks, he asked, "Ready to order?"

"I think so," August said, eyeing Sage. He winked as he said, "Ready, babe?"

"Uh, yeah," she said, sounding caught off guard. It made him want to laugh. She was the one who wanted to put on a show. Sage scanned the menu before looking up at Gavin. "I'll have the salmon sandwich and the truffle fries."

"Fancy," August said.

"It's just a sandwich and fries," Sage said, rolling her eyes.

"A fancy salmon sandwich and fries with truffle oil. Only the best for my little witch," he teased.

Gavin chuckled softly. "My dad calls that the bougie meal on the menu."

"He does not," Sage insisted. "Does he? I'm not bougie. I just like salmon."

"There's nothing wrong with being bougie, babe." August handed his menu to Gavin and said, "I'll have the short rib."

"That comes with goat cheese polenta," Sage said pointedly. "That's way more bougie than a sandwich and fries."

August reached out and slipped his fingers through hers. "I guess we're the perfect pair then, aren't we?"

"So, you are together," Gavin said, eyeing their connected hands. His eyebrows were high on his forehead, and he looked to be not only surprised but a little confused. "Looks like I missed quite a bit while I was in Salem."

"Not that much," August said. "This is sort of new."

"Is it?" Gavin asked, glancing back and forth between the two of them.

"Why are you looking at us like that?" August asked, annoyed that his friend was acting as if he and Sage were the last two people he'd expected to end up dating.

"Uh, sorry," Gavin said, his cheeks turning a faint shade of pink. "It's just that I never expected you to end up with a… um… Befana witch."

"Is there something wrong with dating a Befana witch?" Sage asked, her voice suddenly cold.

"Of course not," Gavin said quickly. "It's not you. I just thought that August would end up with a…" He ran a nervous hand through his dark hair. "You know what? It doesn't matter what I thought. I'm sorry. I shouldn't make assumptions." He hurried away from the table so quickly one would have thought someone had lit a fire under his ass.

"What the hell was that about?" Sage asked, still staring after Gavin.

August sat back in his chair. When he finally spoke, his voice was flat. "He probably thinks you're out of my league."

Sage, who'd just taken a sip of her beer, sputtered. "Out of your league? What does that even mean? There's no hierarchy here in Befana Bay."

"Be serious, Sage," August said, amused. "Of course there is. The founding families will always be more respected. It just comes with the territory. Not only do you have the history, but you're more powerful as well. People are always going to think that the guy who works odd jobs and has an eccentric family is never going to be good enough for Befana royalty."

"That's ridiculous. I'm not better than anyone else," she insisted. Then her expression softened, and she lowered her voice as she added, "And you... Well, I've never met anyone more special than you."

"Did you just say I'm special?" he asked, not entirely sure he'd heard her correctly.

"You heard me." She took a long sip of her beer.

Warmth spread through August's chest as he took in the compliment. He was used to being liked by the people around him. Friendships came easy to him, especially when he was always the guy everyone could count on. But no one had ever called him special or looked at him like they could see past all his baggage that he tried so hard to keep carefully hidden. Like they could really see the man behind the guy who was always ready to lend a helping hand.

He cleared his throat. "Thank you."

She gave him a shy smile as her cheeks turned pink. "You're welcome."

He decided in that moment that there was nothing better

than seeing her flustered. He'd do everything in his power to make her blush every chance he got.

"So," she said, clearing her throat. "I guess now that my grandmother and the coven are taking care of the magic in the bay, we can get back to worrying about having fun. Right?"

August took a swallow of beer as he studied her. "Your grandmother said your powers will come back when you're truly happy."

"Yeah."

"I know we told your grandmother we're dating, and you want to keep that going for a while so she doesn't find out we lied, and that's fine. I'm happy to go to Sunday tarot and put on a show when we're out and about, but I don't want you to feel obligated to spend more time with me. Only if you really want to."

Sage tightened her grip on her beer glass, raised it up, and downed a long gulp. When she placed it back on the table, she stared him in the eye and said, "I want to."

Her words made his stomach flip, and he felt his body heat with nerves. Why did he suddenly feel like some sort of awkward teenager asking a girl out for the first time? He took his own swig of beer and then cleared his throat. "Fun it is. When are you free next?"

She chuckled to herself. "Uh, tonight? We could take a walk down by the water. I always love the way the bay looks at sunset."

He grimaced. "I'd love nothing more than to do that, but I have a prior commitment. Can we do the sunset tomorrow night?"

"Sure. Yeah. I mean of course you're busy." She let out a self-deprecating laugh. "I can't remember a time I had to check my calendar to see if I was free. I think I've trained my friends and family to never make plans with me because I'm always working. No wonder my grandmother zapped my magic."

"Hey," he said softly. "There's nothing wrong with being passionate about your work. Just because you've been focused on that doesn't mean your grandmother should have interfered by messing with your magic."

"She meant well." Sage traced the rim of her glass with her forefinger, not looking at him.

Ah hell. He'd meant to give her support. Show her that someone was taking her side. Not make her feel like he was insulting her grandmother, the only parent figure she had left. "I know she did. I just think there was probably a better way to get her point across. Just my opinion."

Sage snorted. "You think so? Do you know how long she's been trying to get me out of the shop? I believe it started about six months after I opened the doors. So a good ten years. I think maybe she was just exasperated with me."

"Are you telling me you haven't been on a date in ten years?" he asked, only partly teasing.

"No!" She sat back and shook her head at him. "I've dated. Some. It's been a while. I also get together with my sisters once a week for drinks. Okay, lately it's been more like once a month. We've just all been busy."

"All right. I believe you," he said with a laugh. "How about this? For the next month, we'll do all the things you like to do, try some things on your to-do list, and I'll take you along for some things you never *knew* you wanted to do. There's no way your fun-o-meter won't be bursting. When that happens, surely your magic will be back in full force."

She let out a slow breath. "I sure hope so." She sat back, her eyes narrowed slightly. "You know what, August West?"

"What's that, Sage Easton?"

"I'm not as boring as my grandmother thinks I am." There was a glint in her eye when she added, "What do you say that in return for you showing me a good time, I show you a few things?"

A flash of heat hit him like a lightning bolt, and August had to restrain himself from jumping up, pulling her out of her chair, and kissing the ever-loving daylights out of her. Show him a few things, indeed. He tamped down his out-of-control libido and tried his best to sound as casual as possible. "I'm game if you are."

She held her glass up for a toast.

August mimicked the movement.

When she touched her beer to his, she said, "To having all the fun in all the ways possible."

Speechless, he nodded and downed the rest of his beer, hoping the liquid would keep him from combusting right there on the patio.

CHAPTER 12

"So, tomorrow then?" Sage asked as they walked out of The Salt Circle. "I'll be in the store until about six. Can we meet there?" Even though Sage's magic was on the fritz, she still had a shop to run. There were orders to be packed and inventory to be restocked. Thankfully, she'd been gearing up for the spring and summer season and still had enough pieces to fill her shelves, but if her magic didn't come back soon, she was going to have to seriously reconsider her product line. Her magical wares would be a thing of the past, and she'd have to pivot to regular vases, glasses, and other household items.

The very thought made her blood run cold. It wasn't that there was anything wrong with those types of pieces, it was just that she'd built her business on the enchanted ones, and if she had to explain to her customers that she was no longer able to make them, she thought it might break her.

"Hey, where'd you go?" August asked as he moved to stand in front of her.

"Huh?" She glanced up into his handsome face and wondered why she'd been so reluctant to befriend him in the past. Had she really been so judgmental about his lifestyle choices? Yes, yes, she had, and she felt a flash of shame wash over her.

"I was telling you that six o'clock is great and asked if you wanted to get dinner, too, but it seems like you didn't hear me," he said, his brow furrowed.

"Sorry." She waved her hands, trying to somehow clear out all of her thoughts and be present in the moment. "I got caught up in thinking about what I need to do at work tomorrow." She gave him a sheepish grin. "You can take the girl out of the office, but... You know how it goes."

He chuckled. "It'll just give me motivation to make sure you disconnect tomorrow night. Dinner?"

"I'd love to." She stared up at him, wondering what he'd do if she leaned in and—

"Sage?" A familiar voice called out.

She glanced over her shoulder and spotted her sister Prim waving at her. She was flanked by their other two sisters, Lily and Indigo.

"Hey!" Prim waved. "We've been looking for you."

"Give me just a minute." She held up one finger and turned back to August.

August was checking his watch. "I need to pick up my SUV from your grandmother's and get going so I'm not late for my function." He peered at her sisters. "Think one of them can give you a ride home?"

"Of course," she said automatically. Even if they couldn't, her home was only a couple of miles north of town. She could walk if need be.

He eyed her sisters one more time and then smiled mischievously before he leaned in and gave her a lingering kiss.

Sage's arms went around his neck as she leaned into him, ready to open her mouth to welcome the taste of him. But before she could, he pulled back, winked, and then strode off, leaving her with tingling lips and a fluttering heart.

"Woohoo!" one of her sisters called while another let out a piercing whistle. She was too busy watching August walk away to turn around and see who the catcallers were, but if she had to guess, she'd lay bets on Lily and Indigo. Prim was more reserved than the other two.

"Sage," Indigo said in a loud whisper as she moved in right behind her sister. "What is going on with the hot jack-of-all-trades? Have you decided to make him your boy-toy?"

Sage turned around and rolled her eyes at her oldest sister. Indigo was two years older than her, and of the four of them, she was the most vivacious. The one always ready to drop everything and be someone's partner in crime. Honestly, it was part of the reason everyone loved her so much. In fact, fun just might be Indigo's middle name. Sage wondered why she hadn't just asked her sister to help her let her hair down. But when she licked her lips and remembered the tingle of August's kiss, she had to wonder if deep down she'd secretly *wanted* to spend time with August. She wasn't sure she wanted to know the answer.

Prim pressed a hand to her mouth and stifled her laughter. Her blond hair swept over her face as she turned, trying to hide her amusement.

Lily, who could have been Prim's twin, stepped up on the other side of Sage and slipped her arm through hers. "It looks like things with August have heated up considerably. Please tell me you spent the night with him last night."

Indigo tossed her raven-black hair behind her and hooted

with laughter, while Prim bit her bottom lip and stared at Sage with expectant eyes, clearly waiting for the details.

"Oh my gods!" Sage threw her hands up. "Of course I didn't spend the night with August. Would you three calm down. We're just... hanging out. That's all."

"That's not all you're doing," Indigo said with one raised eyebrow. "We saw that smooch. You can call it whatever you want, but Mr. Helpful wants to help you right out of your pants."

"Okay. That's enough," Sage said, her cheeks burning with heat. "That was just..." She shrugged and raised her hands in an I-give-up motion.

"You told Grandmother that you're dating," Prim said quietly. "That's not exactly 'hanging out.'"

"Really? You're dating?" Lily asked, suddenly serious. "I thought he was just being your fun coach. If—"

"If she wanted a fun coach," Indigo said, standing with her hands on her small waist, "she'd have come to me, wouldn't she?" Their oldest sister frowned at Sage, looking put out. "You know you could have just called or texted, or heck, even sent up a smoke signal. It's not like you don't know where to find me."

"Don't be mad," Sage said, wrapping her arm around her sister's shoulders. "The fun coach thing sort of just happened. August just happened to be there when I broke down on the side of the road, and when I ripped my skirt, he helped me find something else to wear. One thing led to another and the next thing I knew, he was at the ball and we had plans for him to show me how to have fun after my magic didn't come back on its own."

"Aww, Indigo, don't pout," Lily added, giving her a sly grin.

"You know you'd choose a hottie like August over us to have some fun with any day of the week."

"And twice on Fridays," Indigo said. "In fact, if I hadn't been dating Skunk Face for the past two years, I'd have already made him my sloppy seconds."

"Indy," Sage said, crossing her arms over her chest. "Could you just not."

Indigo peered at her, recognition dawning in her gaze. "Sorry, sis. I didn't realize it was like that."

"If you weren't so busy thinking about taking him to bonetown, you'd have seen that Sage really likes him," Lily said, mimicking Sage's stance. She was the youngest sister and had the type of relationship with Indigo that let her get away with calling out their older sister without annoying her. But if it were Sage? Forget it. Indigo would just dig in her heels.

"I don't like him," Sage lied. "I mean, we're just friends. Sort of."

All three of her sisters laughed.

Finally, Lily took her by the arm and said, "Come on. Grandmother sent us to get you. She's summoned us to meet her at the house."

"She's back already?" Sage asked, surprised. It hadn't been that long since she and August has left her. She glanced at her watch and was surprised to see they'd spent almost three hours on the patio at The Salt Circle.

"Back?" Indigo asked. "Back from where? Doesn't she always host tea on Sunday afternoons?"

"She does but..." Sage grimaced. "There's a problem with the bay's magic. She and the elders were going to go deal with it. I don't think tea happened today."

"Wait, what do you mean there's something wrong with the bay's magic?" Indigo demanded.

Sage told them all about her morning with August and how the matriarch of the orcas had warned him.

Indigo's deep blue eyes went wide as worry claimed her face. "Are the orcas in danger?"

"I think so," Sage admitted with a tiny nod. "If the magic of the bay dies, who knows what it will do to the ecosystem."

Indigo grabbed Sage's hand and led the four of them toward the large Victorian that overlooked the town.

CHAPTER 13

THE HOUSE WAS LIT with thousands of tiny twinkle lights, and the gargoyle statue that sat guarding the door nodded at them as soon as Indigo climbed the porch stairs. Magic appeared, covering his stone form, and then the front door creaked open, welcoming them to their grandmother's home.

"Fancy," Indigo said as she walked into the house. "It's not every day we get a gargoyle's welcome."

"Definitely not," Lily added.

The gargoyle guarded the house, keeping a watchful eye at all times, but he rarely came to life these days. That only happened when Bethany thought the occasion called for a special welcoming.

"I wonder what that's all about," Prim said, clutching Sage's arm. "I don't think Goyle has acknowledged my presence in at least five years. Not since Grandmother hosted that All Hallows' Eve that one year and went all out to impress every witch within five counties."

Sage fought back a grimace. That was yet another night she'd bailed on due to work. She couldn't even recall what her work emergency was, just that she'd let down her family by not showing up for one of their most sacred holidays. No wonder her grandmother had felt the need to strip her of her power. Sage was still angry at the violation, but she could at least admit that her grandmother had a point.

The four of them filed into the formal living room, where their grandmother sat in an antique wing chair, crocheting a delicate shimmering black shawl.

"Hello, my lovelies," Bethany said, setting her project aside and rising to her feet. She was wearing a flowing black skirt and a deep violet tunic that was covered in lace. Her lace-up, high-heeled boots had intricate silver scrolls embossed on the fine black leather. Her look, right down to the pentacle hanging around her neck, was every inch the leader of a powerful coven.

"Grandmother," Indigo said and leaned in to give her a hug. "You look lovely this evening."

"Thank you, my dear." Bethany gave her a kiss on the cheek and then moved on to hug each of her granddaughters.

When it was Sage's turn, she couldn't help but notice the fatigue in her grandmother's dark green eyes. She was pale, and there was a slight tremor as she raised her arms to embrace her granddaughter. Sage held on for longer than her sisters, willing her younger energy into the older woman. It was rare for Bethany to look so worn out. That only happened when she was wielding powerful magic. Like the kind that it would take to heal the bay. "Are you all right?" Sage whispered in Bethany's ear.

"I am," Bethany whispered back. When she let go of Sage, she gave her a tired smile. "Just a little worn out. Nothing a little energy potion won't fix."

Sage took her by the hand and led her over to the settee.

"Come on. Sit down. We want to hear all about your afternoon. What happened?"

Bethany sank down onto the green velvet couch and waved for her granddaughters to join her.

Sage took the wing chair closest to the settee and reached over to take her grandmother's hand. Bethany tightened her grip around Sage's fingers, holding on as if she needed someone to help steady her.

Indigo took her place next to Bethany, while Lily and Prim took the other two free chairs.

Sage cleared her throat. "It looks like the coven had their work cut out for them today."

Bethany let out a huff of humorless laughter. "You could say that. The amount of power we needed to restore the bay was incredible." She raised her other hand, showing them that she still had a slight tremor. "I can't remember the last time a combined spell drained me this much."

"Gran," Indigo said, looking pained. "Don't you think maybe it's time to start slowing down when it comes to the coven?"

"Slow down?" Bethany flinched as if she'd been struck. "You aren't suggesting that I just throw in my amulet and do what... Organize corn hoe games at the assisted living place in Queenston?"

"Corn hoe?" Lily asked with an amused smile. "What's that? When men throw themselves at women instead of the traditional corn hole game with bean bags and wooden boards?"

Bethany snickered. "The corn hoe game does sound like a lot more fun."

"No doubt," Indigo agreed.

Prim rolled her eyes and shook her head.

"I doubt our grandmother is ever going to be ready to hang up her amulet," Lily said diplomatically.

"You're probably right about that, Lily," Bethany said, straightening her shoulders and staring Indigo down with an air of authority. "I've been the coven leader for nearly three decades. I'm not giving it up now, especially after our bay was targeted."

"Of course not, Gran." Sage squeezed her hand, showing her support. In her opinion, now was not the time to talk to Bethany Befana about taking a step down. There was no doubt she'd wielded an impressive amount of magic, and although she was tired, she was immensely proud of her work. It was an integral part of who her grandmother was, both to the town and to herself.

"Thank you, sweet girl." Bethany gave Sage a warm smile.

"Tell us what happened," Prim said in her calm, quiet way. Sage knew that her younger sister worried about their grandmother, but she was also in awe of her. Whenever the coven got together to cast fantastical spells, Prim often asked to go witness, and if she couldn't, she wanted every last detail.

Bethany let go of Sage's hand and reached behind her, grabbing the leather-bound spell book that had a carving of a primrose on it. "It's all in here." She patted the book and then offered it to Prim. "I wrote it down as soon as I got home."

Prim's face lit up with delight as she took the book. "You should have rested instead of documenting everything right away, but I really do appreciate it."

"The best time to record a coven spell is right after it takes place. You know that." She gave Prim the tiniest of winks.

"You're the best." Prim got up and then bent down to give her gran a hug. The pair held on for a long moment until finally Bethany let out a small chuckle and gently pulled away. "Do you want to hear about this or not?"

"I do," Prim said and reclaimed her seat.

All three of Sage's sisters were on the edge of their seats, like they always were when Bethany recounted the details of the coven's work. Sage was more interested in making sure her grandmother was mentally and physically okay after expelling so much power.

As Bethany started to detail the chant they'd used to call the earth's power to them, Sage got up and moved into the kitchen. No one paid any attention to her, as they all knew she'd be back shortly. It was the pattern. Her sisters learned about the inner workings of the coven, while Sage took care of their grandmother.

The truth was, Sage had no interest in being part of the coven. If they called on her for help, she'd be there in a heartbeat. But in reality, she'd rather be in her shop making her magical creations instead of overseeing the magical wellness of the entire town. She rummaged through her grandmother's cabinets until she found the special tea leaves she'd left there and then got to work.

Ten minutes later, Sage walked back into the living room, carrying a tray of restorative tea and a variety of fancy cookies. She set it down on the coffee table, and without a word, she handed each of her sisters and her grandmother a teacup.

Her sisters barely acknowledged her, but Bethany paused in the middle of her story and met Sage's gaze. "You remind me so much of your mother. Always nurturing. I think we all take that for granted sometimes." She took a sip of her tea, and immediately her eyes brightened. "You're always so busy at your shop. I forgot just how talented you are with these tea leaves."

Sage stared at her grandmother, dumbfounded. She thought Sage was nurturing? Sage didn't know if she'd go that far.

"Stop," her grandmother ordered her with a frown.

"Stop what?" Sage asked, glancing around, only to find each of her sisters sitting still and staring at her.

"Your self-doubts," Bethany said. "It's true. You're always the one taking care of anyone who needs it in this family. If there is one thing you'll stop working for, it's to be there if one of us needs you for anything. Just take the compliment and say thank you."

"Thank you," Sage parroted.

Her grandmother's posture relaxed. "Was that so hard?"

Sage just shrugged one shoulder. It was hard to take a compliment when you'd been told you were doing life wrong ever since you graduated from high school, but Sage accepted that her grandmother was trying. Their relationship had been strained at best since Bethany zapped Sage's magic. Sage was happy to try to put that entire thing behind them. And she would, too, if only her magic wasn't still MIA.

"Is this elderberry?" Prim asked after taking a sip of the tea.

"It is. With a healthy dose of echinacea. It's both restorative and healing," Sage said.

"Lucky for you," Indigo told Prim with a snicker. "Maybe tomorrow you'll wake up and that pimple in the middle of your forehead will be gone."

Prim shook her head slightly, and for a moment, Sage thought her sister was going to let that comment slide.

But when Indigo reached for a cookie, Prim pointed her pinky finger at her and sent a zap of magic in her direction. The magic obliterated the butter cookie before Indigo could get it to her mouth.

Indigo sat there, stunned, and then turned her steely gaze on her younger sister. "You did not want to do that."

"Oh, I think she did," Lily said with a snicker. "After that comment, you're lucky she didn't take a finger off."

Prim held her fist up and Lily bumped it with her own. Even though all four sisters had been close growing up. Lily and Prim, who were only ten months apart, really were more like twins than anything else. The bond between them was something no one else seemed to be able to penetrate.

"Oh no. You two aren't ganging up on me." Indigo turned to Sage. "I'm gonna need you to help me take them down."

Sage laughed. "Take them down? What are you planning, mud wrestling?"

Indigo's face crinkled in disgust. "Who do you think I am? As if I'd ever be caught dead rolling around in mud. No, we're going to challenge them to a race."

Lily shot out of her chair and raised her arm in the air. "I'm in!"

"You don't even know what we're racing," Sage said, sitting back in her chair.

Indigo scoffed. "Are you serious? Is there any way to race other than—"

All three sisters as well as their grandmother cut Indigo off as they cried, "On broomsticks!"

CHAPTER 14

"This isn't fair," Lily complained as Indigo started to hand out broomsticks to each of them. They'd moved out to the backyard and were standing on a separate deck that was sandwiched between two flower beds and was the perfect spot for whale watching. Lily inspected the nondescript wooden broom her sister had given her. "How do we know you didn't choose the minivan version for me and Prim but the sportscar version for you and Sage?"

"Do you really think so little of me?" Indigo asked, a heavy dose of indignation in her tone.

"Yes," Prim and Lily said at the same time, making their grandmother laugh.

The matriarch was sitting on the outdoor sectional with her feet up, watching her granddaughters' shenanigans.

Indigo turned to Sage. "Can you believe this abuse? They act like we don't remember the time they spiked our hot cocoas, causing us to sound like chipmunks on New Year's Eve. Our dates bailed out at the last minute, and both of us ended up spending the night fending off that casting director for that kids' movie. What was it called? Buck & Bunny?"

Sage cackled. "Yes. I swear that movie still sounds like a porn flick."

"Imagine our voices in that thing." Indigo made a couple of high-pitched cries of pleasure before erupting into laughter and collapsing onto the sectional next to their grandmother.

"All right! All right!" Lily said, throwing her hands up. "That might have been an error in judgment. If I had to do it again, I'd spike the cocoa with something that caused flatulence. Then instead of ruining your New Year's plans, we'd have had hilarious memories for the rest of our lives. If there'd been video..."

Sage and Indigo glanced at each other and grimaced.

"And you people wonder why I spend so much time in my studio," Sage said with her arms crossed over her chest. "Flatulence? Really, Lily?"

Lily only laughed harder.

Meanwhile, Prim walked over to Indigo and said, "The only way to make it fair is if you pick your broom last." Then she went down the line, grabbing the neck of each broom until she picked the sleek silver one that had black inlay on the handle. "Sage, you pick next. Then Lily, and Indigo last."

"I just need the one that's spelled with the most magic," Sage said. "Since my magic is still MIA, I just want something that's going to keep me in the air." She turned to Indigo. "Which one?"

"Zzzpt!" Prim said, putting her fingers up to Indigo's lips. "No helping. She has to pick her own broom."

"That's so unfair," Sage complained. "You two can use your magic to assess what you're getting into with a broom. I just have to guess."

"It's not like you haven't ever ridden a broom, Sage," Lily said, sounding exasperated. "Indigo didn't just open the shop a week ago."

No, she hadn't. It had been their parents' shop before their deaths. Bethany had made sure to keep the store running until either the girls decided to sell it or one of them took it over. Right after Indigo graduated from high school, she'd insisted they'd never sell the shop. It could either be a family run store, or she'd take it over. Sage had opened a glass studio. Prim, who was skilled with fibers, took over managing the legendary yarn shop in town. And then there was Lily. She was a writer. She had a weekly satire column in the paper that was titled, *Ask Endora*. All of her responses to the people who sent in their relationship questions were sarcastic, over the top, and just plain bad advice. It was so popular, even book publishers were sniffing around. But as far as Sage new, Lily hadn't ever written anything longer than 500 words. So who knew what would happen, but Sage was rooting for her.

"Are you gonna pick a broom or what?" Lily asked Sage, tapping her foot.

"I'm on it," Sage said, still annoyed that she'd have to pick one and cross her fingers it was well suited for those without power. All of them were spelled; it was just that some were suited for those with magic and some for those without. And even after all these years, Sage still didn't know the difference. If she had her magic, she could tell. She walked over and grabbed the broomstick that had bright red bristles just because she thought it looked pretty. "Okay, I'm done."

"Great choice," Indigo whispered to her.

Sage let out a sigh of relief. The last thing she needed was to be dumped off her broom in the middle of the bay.

Lily squealed when she chose her broom. And

unsurprisingly, Indigo grimaced as she took the remaining crooked broom that looked more like a prop from a movie than a real broomstick a modern witch might ride.

Cackling, Lily moved past them toward the edge of the deck. She tossed her long blond hair over one shoulder as she glanced back and said, "I knew you were trying to pull a fast one on us."

"I was not, I just— You know what? Never mind." Indigo walked over to Sage. "Do you want to trade?"

Sage blinked at her. "Why? You told me I made an excellent choice."

"You did. It's the fastest model we have, so obviously, it's great for our team. I just thought you'd feel safer on the workhorse."

The broomstick in Sage's hold started to vibrate. The kind of vibrating they did when a witch was testing the broom's power. If her power was still neutralized, Sage should not feel it. She glanced up, finding her grandmother watching her.

"I told you it'd come back when you were truly happy." Bethany waved a hand in front of her, palm up. "This, my loves, is what being a Befana is all about." She stood and walked over to the porch, and in seconds the older witch was straddling a broom. "I hope you're ready," she called as she snapped her fingers, causing the broom to lift her into the air. A sage green flag decorated with an assortment of flowers appeared out of thin air. Bethany mounted it on the handle of the broom and then shot through the air, shouting over her shoulder, "Whoever catches me and gets my flag, wins."

No one hesitated. All four mounted their brooms within seconds and took off after her.

It was no surprise when Indigo took the lead. Despite her

minivan model of a broom, she had the most experience riding and was currently flying circles around all three of her sisters.

Sage, however, was struggling. She'd gotten used to having no magic over the past few weeks. Now that it was surging through her veins, she was having trouble controlling it. The magic was too unwieldy, and she had the impression if someone with experience were riding her broom, they'd really be giving Indigo a run for her money.

"Let's go, Sage!" Indigo cried as she whipped by.

The broom shot forward all on its own. Or maybe it had been Indigo's command. Either way, Sage was barely holding on for dear life. She heard her younger sisters behind her, yelling for her to give them a break.

Ha. Fat chance.

This was war. And after the last three weeks of frustration, she was ready to let off some steam. She'd used magic on a daily basis prior to the curse. She knew how to manipulate it. Why was she holding back now? She didn't know. "Now or never, Sage," she whispered to herself and then let her magic intermingle with the broom's.

The broom with the red bristles was a thing of beauty. It flew with an ease Sage had never known before. She briefly wondered how much the broom cost, because if it felt that way to fly every time, she just might make it a daily thing. There was no time to think about what she might do. Not when she'd just dashed right by Indigo, releasing both hands from the broom and giving her sister two thumbs-up.

"No hands, Sage?" Indigo called after her, and then whatever she said next was drowned out by a fierce gust of wind.

Sage held on tightly to the broom, leaning in close to lie on it as it rolled several times due to the unexpected massive wind gusts that had just taken over the bay. It took all of Sage's concentration to keep her magic connected to the broom's so that she wouldn't end up fish food.

Just ahead, Sage spotted her grandmother sitting atop her broom in a small windless bubble, idling as if she were waiting for something, or someone.

Well, of course she was. She was waiting for one of them to come get her flag.

Sage glanced back at her sisters. They were all still behind her. And without hesitation, Sage shot forward, aiming to get the flag in one shot. But as soon as she reached her grandmother's small bubble, she felt rather than heard the high-pitched call of one of the orcas. She glanced down and spotted a young one that couldn't have been more than a handful of years old, thrashing about, no doubt agitated.

Worry washed over Sage and just like that, her magic disappeared again. In the blink of an eye, she lost control of the broom and spun in a spiral all the way down until she splashed into the water, the chill hitting her like a ton of bricks.

She hit so hard she wasn't even sure she could breathe. But before she could make any sort of assessment of her overall wellbeing, the orcas were back, and the one that had been thrashing about swam up close to Sage and eyed her with suspicion. Then without warning, he dove and came up right underneath her. She was splayed out on the back of the orca as he took her back home.

CHAPTER 15

AUGUST STOOD IN HIS GARAGE, holding a paintbrush and staring at the hot mess of a canvas in front of him. He'd turned half of his garage space into a studio not long after he'd moved in and spent a lot of time out there when he needed to clear his mind. This morning, however, no matter how hard he tried to concentrate, he just couldn't seem to get his creative energy to cooperate. Usually he knew exactly what he wanted to paint. But today, it was as if his mind kept glitching and the only thing he could focus on was his father when he'd been out back stealing magic from the bay. And before he knew it, the image in front of him had started to look like his backyard with magic clinging to the bay.

That wasn't what he wanted to paint.

He came to his studio to get his mind off things, not immerse himself into memories of events he'd rather forget.

Frustrated, he swiped a streak of black paint across the canvas. An intense sense of wrongness hit him in the solar plexus, causing him to involuntarily drop the brush. The sound of the wood bouncing off the concrete rang in his ears, breaking the silence. He froze, his eyes darting around the garage, searching for the source of the nausea-inducing energy that made him want to hurl.

"What the hell," he said under his breath.

His phone suddenly started blaring "Highway to Hell," startling him so bad he nearly jumped out of his boots. He pressed a hand to his pounding heart and let out a long breath. *Witch's balls*, he thought and shook his head. He'd almost had heart failure just because his ringer was turned to a level that would rattle the windows. The phone started going off again, and he grabbed it.

Silas Ansell's name filled the screen. August quickly answered. "Hey, Si. What's up?"

"Where are you?" the actor asked.

"In my studio. Where are you?"

"At your front door. Got a minute?" Silas asked.

"Yeah. Be right there." August ended the call, hastily cleaned the paint off his hands, and then hurried to open the front door. "Hey, if it isn't two of my favorite people," he said, painting on a bright smile. When Levi frowned at him, August knew the spirit witch could see right through him.

"Everything okay?" Levi asked, stepping closer to peer at August.

"Yeah, I just…" He ran a hand through his hair, wondering what to say. That he'd been creeped out by absolutely nothing tangible and that his ring tone had taken a couple years off his life? "I'm just a little out of sorts this morning. Nothing to worry about." He took a step back and opened the door wide, inviting his friends in. "Come in. I'll make us some coffee."

The couple followed August into the house as he led them to the sun-filled kitchen.

"Take a seat," August said as he busied himself with the coffee maker.

Neither of the men paid any attention to him. Instead, Silas raided his refrigerator, finding a tube of cinnamon rolls. He set the oven to preheat and went to work on arranging them in a pan. Levi grabbed mugs and found the fancy creamer and sugar bowl he'd inherited from his grandmother.

"Were you guys just hungry?" August asked, amused. "You know, you could just try grocery shopping for once."

Levi leaned against the counter and shoved his hands into the pockets of his jeans. "I tried that. Silas still managed to coax me into eating out almost every day. The man is addicted to the restaurants here."

"Is it my fault the food's just that good?" Silas asked. "You can't blame me. You did try those apple dumplings at Baker's Spell, right?"

"I tried them. But we don't have to have them for breakfast *every* morning, do we?"

Silas scoffed and pressed a hand to his heart. "You wound me." He turned to August. "Back me up here? Wouldn't you eat there every morning if it was right next door?"

"Probably," August admitted. Baker's Spell was a staple in Befana Bay. Their goods were made with local ingredients and infused with a tiny bit of magic that was said to help your day go smoother. It was like an intention spell. Basically, if you wish it, you can manifest it into existence. It wouldn't work on things like, *I wish I'd win the super jackpot over at the casino.* But the magic did wonders for helping a person do well at an audition or job interview. It was no wonder Baker's Spell always had a line halfway around the block.

"Okay, stop harassing me," Silas said to Levi and then turned to August. "I have a business proposition for you and didn't want you to be making any decisions on an empty stomach. Judging by your disheveled appearance and the paint dried on your hands, I'm guessing it's been a while since you've eaten anything."

August thought back, trying to remember the last thing he'd eaten. Besides the granola bar he'd hastily put away while he been driving back from his appointment in Port Townsend the night before, the last time he'd eaten was at The Salt Circle with Sage. His fingers ached to pull out his phone and call her, just to hear her voice.

"Earth to August," Silas said, waving a hand to get his attention. "Are you okay, man?"

"Yeah," August said, shaking his head to clear his thoughts. "Sorry. I guess it has been a while since I've eaten. Low blood sugar is making me spacey."

"Never fear, we'll get that taken care of." Levi opened the fridge and pulled out some eggs and bacon and made himself at home, cooking them a real breakfast while the cinnamon rolls baked.

Silas poured them each a cup of coffee and then motioned for August to join him at the table. As he was taking his seat, Silas called to Levi, "Let me know if you need any help."

Levi waved him off. "I've got it. No one wants burned eggs and undercooked bacon." Levi winked at his fiancé.

"It's not like I don't try," Silas told August. "I think I just have some mental block when it comes to cooking."

August snorted. Mental block. Sure. "For someone who can seem to play almost any role, I find it interesting that you can't seem to slip into one of basic cook."

"Right? It's perplexing." He smirked and took a sip of his coffee. "Anyway, let's get down to business."

August gestured with his mug for the other man to continue.

Silas set his mug down and jumped right in. "I want to talk about *Keating River*."

"Your TV show?" August asked, raising a curious eyebrow. Silas wrote a script based on his and Levi's love story. He'd almost sold it to an established studio, but just before he signed, he backed out and it was now being produced by the paranormal romance writer, Miranda Moon. She and her husband formed their own production company so that creators would have more control.

"Yes." Silas nodded. "We finally decided on that name as a nod to Keating Hollow even though both the main characters travel a lot. As it turns out, most of the scenes will be in Keating Hollow, so it works out. Anyway, we're getting to the point where we need to start hiring."

August sat back in his chair and nodded. "Sure. Do you need some names or recommendations of people? I've got a list of some of the best in the business. Or at least the best who usually film up here."

"Sure, that'd be great," Silas said. "I'd love to see who you enjoyed working with. But that's not all I need from you."

That wasn't a surprise. Silas had been in the business for years. He likely had his own list of people he'd pull from. "Okay. How can I help?"

"I'd like you to be our production manager. I don't want just anyone in that role. I want someone I can trust, someone who knows how to get things done. That's you."

August stared at his friend, slightly dumbfounded. When the shock started to wear off, he said, "That position usually requires someone with knowledge in finance and accounting. I don't have a degree in either."

"But you have the experience," Silas said pointedly. "Don't think I didn't notice you doing the PM's job for him while we were filming that rom-com last fall. He could barely figure out the tip on his takeout, much less make sure the movie stayed on budget. I don't care about degrees. Neither does Miranda. We care about who can get the job done and will do it while respecting everyone working for them. Everyone who works with you loves you. Me and Levi included. Do you know how rare that is? I'd really love it if the set of *Keating River* is as harmonious as possible. The kind of set that everyone wants to work on. I know that can only happen with the right people in charge."

"Filming will be in Keating Hollow, right?" August asked hesitantly.

"Yes."

"How many seasons and how long do you anticipate filming to go on? Three, four months? Or longer?"

"We're hoping for five months, but it could be as long as six. We're going for a sixteen-episode season."

August blew out a long breath. There was a reason he usually only worked as a production assistant. It meant he had a lot of flexibility to take care of all his other commitments. Namely one. The one that took him to Port Townsend once a week. Sure, he'd worked on that movie in Keating Hollow last fall, but it had only been for a couple of months, and his grandma Serena had been in town. She'd taken over his weekly run. But he couldn't ask her to do that for five or six months. Not with her travel schedule.

"What's the issue, August?" Silas asked, studying him. "Is it the added responsibility? Because if you're worried you don't have what it takes to do the job, well, I'm here to tell you you're wrong. I know you can. I've seen it with my own eyes."

"It's not that. Or not only that." He blew out a long breath. "Listen, Silas, I really appreciate this offer, but—"

Silas held his hand up, stopping him. "Please don't answer yet. Take some time to think about it. I'll get a contract sent over so you know all the details and can make an informed decision. There's no rush here. We're still working on the timeline and nailing down the actors."

"Yeah, okay. I can do that." August shook his head, frustrated with himself. A good friend has just offered him an amazing opportunity, and instead of thanking him, he'd acted put out as if it were even a burden to consider such a thing. He eyed Silas and gave the actor a ghost of a smile. "I really do appreciate the offer. And your faith in me..."

"I know there's a *but* coming," Silas said with a wry smile. "Do I want to hear it?"

August chuckled. "Maybe? I'm not saying no. I will take my time to think about it."

"Okay, lay it on me." Silas glanced up as Levi appeared, putting breakfast plates in front of both of them.

"Thanks," August said to Levi, wondering how it had come to be that one of the biggest stars in Hollywood was sitting at his table, offering him a dream job, while a major rock star was cooking him breakfast. He turned his attention to Silas and tried to be as honest as possible without breaking anyone's trust. "I really would like to just say yes. Working with you and Miranda sounds like a dream job."

Silas stayed silent, waiting patiently.

Not for the first time, it struck August just how different Silas Ansell was from the many other celebrities he'd met over the years. The man was humble, patient, and really listened to others. Those were some rare traits when it came to Hollywood talent. "There are just other commitments that keep me close to Befana Bay. Commitments that don't have anything to do with my career." A sardonic chuckle escaped his lips before he added, "Or lack of career if I'm being honest."

"You know, most actors take time off between jobs, too. It's not an indication that you don't have a meaningful career," Silas said matter-of-factly. "You and I both know you could work every week of the year if you wanted to."

"He's not wrong," Levi said, taking a seat next to Silas. "Do you think Silas would be here begging you to go to work with him if you weren't the best in the biz?"

"Okay, stop the full court press," August said, feeling even more conflicted than ever. If he thought there was any feasible way to make it work, he'd have said yes in a heartbeat. He knew that working with Silas would not only be the break of a lifetime, but he'd thoroughly enjoy it, too. "I said I'd think it over. You don't need to stroke my ego more."

Levi shrugged. "Just stating facts."

"You guys make a great team," August said as envy seemed to wash over him. He was normally a pretty happy and content guy, but he had to admit that suddenly he felt like he was missing something by not having someone to walk through life with, enjoying both the large and small moments.

"We think so." Silas glanced at Levi, and the two stared at each other, sharing a moment.

August grabbed his empty plate and took it into the kitchen, wanting to let the two men have their private moment. He'd just started loading the dishwasher when Levi appeared beside him and started clearing the counter.

"Oh no," August said. "I've got this. The chef does not clean. Have another cup of coffee and take a seat."

Levi pressed his lips into a thin line and looked as if he was going to argue. But before he could say anything, the buzzer on the oven went off, indicating that the cinnamon rolls were ready. "I'll get them," he said and grabbed an oven mitt before August could even dry his hands.

Twenty minutes later, the three of them were sitting outside, enjoying the view of the Hood Canal while eating their after-breakfast cinnamon rolls.

"I could get used to this," Silas said, licking the icing off his lips.

"Eating cinnamon rolls?" August asked him.

"No," Silas said, shaking his head. "Living here in Befana Bay, right on the water. There's just something about it that soothes the soul."

"So do the mountains," Levi said. "I can't imagine leaving Keating Hollow."

Silas reached over and squeezed Levi's hand. "We'll never leave Keating Hollow, but it might be nice to get a place here, don't you think?"

While the two discussed their future real estate plans, August rose and moved toward the bank that was high above the waterline. He took pains to ignore the scorched earth his father had left after his ill-fated night of magic siphoning, but just as he passed it, that feeling of wrongness he'd felt earlier that morning overtook him again. His head began to spin, and his breakfast was threatening to make a reappearance.

"August?" Levi said from behind him.

"What is it?" August asked, his gaze glued to the burned earth.

"There's someone here who wants to talk to you," Levi said softly, carefully, as if he were stepping on eggshells.

August slowly turned around and let out a small gasp when his gaze landed on the ghostly apparition. "Grandma?"

CHAPTER 16

"Hɪ, Sᴏɴɴʏ Bᴏʏ," his grandmother, Addie West, said, her expression full of love.

"Grandma?" he asked, his voice barely a whisper. He moved closer to her, moving slowly as if he might be in danger of scaring her off.

"I've missed you." Her eyes were watery as she watched him.

"I've missed you, too," he choked out. "Where have you been all this time?"

She stretched her arms out to the side and glanced around the property. "Right here waiting. It took you long enough to move in. I thought Miss Penny would never leave."

He let out a huff of laughter. "I'm here now."

"You certainly are," she said with a nod. Her expression sobered and her ghostly form rose a few feet off the ground until she was hovering right over the scorched earth. When she spoke again, her voice was thready and haunting. "Beware of those seeking to take what doesn't belong to them. History will repeat itself in more ways than one."

August was too stunned to speak as he took in her warning. History would repeat itself? Someone was taking what didn't belong to them? His father's face flashed in his mind, and anger coiled deep in his gut. He focused on his grandmother once more, watching as her translucent form solidified and floated to the ground and turned. "Who's stealing, Grandma? Is it Dad? Is he going to try to steal the bay's magic again?"

His grandmother blinked at him and then glanced around the clearing. "Is Phillip here?"

"No, but he was earlier. He was siphoning magic off the bay."

She pressed her lips into a thin line. It was her look of disapproval. "You tell that son of mine that I don't approve. Do you understand?"

"Sure, but—"

His grandmother's ghostly form faded quickly. She waved and mouthed, *I love you,* and then she was gone.

"Grandma?" August called, but there was no answer. He spun around, looking for her, desperate to get just one more minute with her. But there was no one around except Levi and Silas, standing near the house, waiting.

August hurried over to them. "Can we get her back?"

Levi shook his head. "I don't think so."

"But you're a spirit witch," August said, making it sound like an accusation. "If anyone can summon a spirit, it's a spirit witch."

"It doesn't work that way," Levi said with a sad shake of his head. "I wish it did."

"Dammit!" August stalked his way back up to the house as the shock of seeing his grandmother's ghost faded and anger moved in. There was no mistaking that warning. His father would be back, and now that the magic of the bay was restored, no doubt he'd try to steal it again.

"August!" Levi called, running after him.

"Not now, Levi. I need to find my father."

August strode into his house, his footsteps pounding on the hardwood floors like a man on a mission. He supposed he was. One way or another, he was going to stop his father before he was able to steal the magic from the bay again. He stormed into the kitchen and rummaged around the butcherblock counter that held his unopened mail. When he didn't find his phone, he moved on to checking the table. No phone. "Where is it?"

"Highway to Hell" started blaring from the other room. He hurried into the living room and followed the sound. It was coming from the corner of the couch where he'd tossed it when he greeted Silas and Levi earlier. He grabbed it without even checking the caller ID, found his father's number, and hit Send.

To his surprise, his father answered on the first ring. "August. I've been waiting for this phone call."

"Seriously? After everything you've done, that's what you want to say to me? I tried to get in touch with you all day yesterday," August fumed.

"We need to talk," Phillip said. "And not over the phone. Meet me tonight at seven."

In person worked for August. It would make it easier to restrain his father and haul him into the Befana Bay sheriff's station if there was even a hint of magic siphoning. "Where?"

"The North Star trailhead parking lot on Highway 104." The line went dead before August could even confirm he'd be there.

"That son of a jackhole," he muttered as he stuffed the

phone into his pocket and returned to the kitchen. Running both hands through his hair, he sank into one of the kitchen chairs and hung his head, trying to process everything that had happened that day.

He heard the soft footsteps of his friends and looked up just as Levi pulled out the chair beside him and took a seat. Silas sat on his other side, and some of the dread in August's heart started to fade. The act of them flanking him on both sides made him feel as if he wasn't alone in this, even though he knew there was no way he'd let either of them get involved with his father. August knew from experience that was too dangerous.

"Want to fill us in on what's going on?" Levi asked.

"What's to say? You heard my grandmother's warning," August said.

"I did," Levi said with a nod. "But Silas didn't. He couldn't see or hear her."

August turned his head, eyeing Silas. "Really? You can't see ghosts?"

"I don't know if I can or not. All I can tell for sure is that your grandmother didn't want me to see her for some reason. As for if I'll ever see any other spirits, time will tell, eventually."

"Did you feel her presence?" August asked.

"Yes. Her energy maybe?" Silas said, turning to Levi for confirmation. "It was sweet at first, but then it turned cool, so cold it felt like it was stinging my skin. Then right before she vanished, her energy turned sweet and wistful again, like she really didn't want to leave."

"No nausea?" he asked, pressing a hand to his stomach as the memory of wrongness enveloped him.

"No, why?" Silas asked.

"There was an unwelcome energy present out there," Levi

said as he placed a supportive hand on August's shoulder. "You felt it deeply, didn't you?"

"Yeah. I'm pretty sure it was my father." August wanted to vomit and hurl something priceless at the wall.

"Are you sure?" Levi asked, sounding skeptical.

"I'm sure. That warning was definitely about him. He's already been here this week once to siphon the magic from the bay. He disappeared shortly after that, but he's been too hidden for me to find him. I'm pretty sure that after the coven witches restored the magic in the bay, he's just waiting for his chance to try again."

"And you're going to go meet him?" Levi looked worried. "By yourself?"

"Yes. Tonight."

"I can't let you go alone, August," Levi said. "It's too dangerous."

It was dangerous, but August would never admit that because he was going, and no amount of words or warnings was going to change the fact that he wouldn't subject anyone he knew to his father. August didn't trust him and for good reason. "I'll be fine," August insisted. "He won't hurt me."

Would he, though? August didn't think so. But if he got cagey, anything was possible.

"August, I really don't think that's a good idea," Levi insisted, sounding stronger. "If you're going to meet your father, I want to be there as backup."

"Sorry, Levi. I'm going alone. It's not up for debate."

Levi let out a long sigh of frustration. "Will you at least call and let us know you're safe?"

"I can do that," August said, glancing at the clock. "But first I need to call Sage and break our date," he grumbled.

Silas and Levi shared a look, but August ignored it, walked

into the other room, and called the only person he really wanted to see that night.

"August," she said after she answered, sounding cheerful. "Ready for our date tonight?"

He winced, hating that he was letting her down. "That's the thing," he said, knowing he sounded like a douche canoe. "I'm not going to be able to make it. Can I get a rain check?"

"Rain check? Why?"

"Something's come up. Something unavoidable," he said, glancing at his watch. It was still hours until he had to meet his father, but he knew from experience he needed to get into a better head space. "Can we try for tomorrow?" he asked, deliberately not looping her in on the latest development with his father. He knew she'd want to go and he didn't want to put her in danger. He just had a bad feeling about how it all might go down.

"I can't," she said with a sigh. "I have to model for that art class my grandmother signed me up for."

Some of his irritation faded when he thought of her standing naked in front of an art class, and he asked, "How do I sign up again?"

Sage chuckled into the phone. "Good luck getting a spot. I heard the class sold out."

"Don't worry about me," August said. "I'll find a way."

He always did.

CHAPTER 17

AUGUST PULLED into the dark parking area of the trailhead and grit his teeth. Either his father hadn't arrived yet or he was playing games and had parked where his vehicle wouldn't be spotted. His money was on playing games. That's what he always did, didn't he? It's why he wanted to meet out at a trailhead instead of somewhere sensible like the coffee shop or August's house. Not that he wanted his father to step foot on his property, but at least it would have made more sense than a trailhead three miles off the highway.

He circled the lot and parked so that his SUV was facing the road. If he had to make a quick getaway, at least he'd be prepared. He glanced over at the amulet lying on the passenger seat. It wasn't anything that would help him wield magic. August didn't have that kind of power. But it could act as a shield if anything or anyone attacked him. The idea that his own father might actually attack him made his head pound with tension.

Hadn't his father learned his lesson when it came to casting nefarious spells all those years ago when the worst had happened? There was a reason his grandmother had disinherited her middle son. She'd skipped right over him and given the house to August and left the rest of her assets to her two other sons. Phillip had been left out in the cold. It's why he'd tried so hard to manipulate August into that bad real estate deal.

August checked his watch. His father was ten minutes late.

He grabbed the amulet, climbed out of the SUV, and cautiously walked around the parking lot, making sure his father wasn't waiting in the shadows. When he came up empty, he returned to his SUV and called his father. His number went straight to voice mail. August left a terse message asking where his father was before ending the call.

As the time ticked by, August fumed silently. Finally, when an hour had gone by, he tried his father one last time. No answer. Then he called Levi as he'd promised.

"Finally," Levi said. "Are you all right?"

"Perfectly fine. I canceled my date with Sage just so I could get stood up. He never showed."

"Jackass," Levi muttered over the din in the background.

"You can say that again."

"Where are you headed now? Are you going to try to meet up with Sage?"

August contemplated that. He wanted to see her but decided it wasn't a good idea. He was far too irritated. "Probably not. What I need is a good stiff drink and to unwind. Besides, I'm sure she's already made new plans."

"Come join us. Silas and I are at the Troll Bridge. I'll order you a whiskey so it's ready when you get here."

"I don't think—" August started.

"I'm not taking no for an answer," Levi said. "Get down here and let me and Silas get your mind off things."

August knew he could decline, that no matter what Levi said, he'd understand if August didn't show up. But the truth was he liked having friends who wanted to look out for him. Besides, if he bailed, what was he going to do? Go home, have that drink, and then stew in his anger? It was far better to go see his friends and try to put his father out of his mind until he had time to process. "All right. I'll be there in twenty."

"Your drink will be waiting."

August ended the call and headed back toward town. The Troll Bridge pub was located right next to the Devil's Cauldron Bridge that spanned the bay and led to Crystal Point Island. The Island was populated mostly with summer homes that had been turned into short term rentals. He didn't frequent the pub often, mostly just because it was a few miles out of town. The parking lot was fairly full, and August wondered if there was some sort of event going on.

He let out an audible groan when he recognized the cast from an ongoing television show that filmed in Befana Bay. *Haunted High* must be getting ready to start filming their newest season. He vaguely recalled being asked to work on that show, but he'd politely declined. Calling the star of the show, Walker Wilson, difficult was an understatement. His ego had ballooned at the same rate as his star power. It wasn't shocking. That happened with a lot of newly famous actors in their early twenties, but it did make for an unpleasant work environment.

As he approached the outdoor garden, he spotted the one person he liked on the show. He raised his hand to wave at Nathan but then dropped it when he spotted Walker approach him with his arm around an attractive blond guy who was hanging on his every word. The easy, carefree expression on Nathan's face vanished, and he looked like he wanted to vomit.

Anger sat like a rock in August's gut. What had Walker said to make Nathan's mood change so quickly?

August vaguely recalled that the two had dated during the last season. Walker was bi, and Nathan identified as pan. Nathan was a sensitive soul who was kind to everyone, while Walker was true to his name and walked all over everyone. August was just coming up on them when he heard Walker talking.

"You know, Nathan, you've got to stop with those lovesick eyes. If you keep that up, the tabloids are never going to stop writing about that ridiculous crush you had on me last year."

"Crush?" Nathan parroted, looking as if he'd been gut punched.

Something inside of August snapped and without thinking, he strode over to Nathan and wrapped an arm around his shoulders. "Sorry I'm late, babe. Didn't mean to keep you waiting."

Nathan jerked his head up and stared at him in complete shock.

"Uh-oh, looks like you've got a smudge of something right here." He leaned in, pretending to clean off his cheek as he whispered, "Just go with it." Then he kissed Nathan's temple and turned to Walker, giving him a bright smile. "Hey there. Have we met? You seem familiar."

The actor's face turned bright red as he sputtered, "*You* are with Nathan?"

"Yep." August eyed him and then said, "Oh, I know who you are now."

Walker's expression turned to one of extreme satisfaction.

"You used to date Nathan, right?" He held out his hand to the other man. "I'm August. What was your name again?"

Walker's face turned stony. And without another word to

him or Nathan, the actor grabbed his date's hand and drug him into the pub.

Nathan blew out a long breath. "I can't believe you just did that."

August kept his arm draped over his friend's shoulders and said, "Anything to stick it to that jackass. Are you all right?"

"I am now." Nathan let out a small chuckle. "Thank you. That *jackass* just caught me off guard, otherwise, I'd have never let him get under my skin."

"I know." August glanced into the patio and spotted Walker still watching them. "He's not going to take his eyes off you tonight. Want to keep up the charade?"

Nathan glanced over to where Walker was shooting daggers at them with his eyes. "Thanks, but I don't want to ruin your night. I should probably just go back to the inn and stream old episodes of *Dawson's Creek*."

"Stream what?" August shook his head. "Never mind. Forget that. You're going to come into the pub with me and have a drink with Silas and Levi. If this little display we just put on doesn't get under Walker's skin, seeing you spending the evening with Silas and Levi will."

Nathan's eyes gleamed. "Won't Silas and Levi mind?"

"No. Now come on." August grabbed Nathan's hand and led the way past Walker and his date. He couldn't help but notice the young actor's jaw drop when they sat down at Levi and Silas's table. He couldn't help the smug smile that claimed his lips when Walker started to scowl.

CHAPTER 18

SAGE JUMPED out of her sister's car and waited for Indigo to join her. When August had canceled, Sage had figured she'd catch up on some computer work. She was ten minutes into analyzing her inventory when she'd slammed her laptop shut and grabbed her phone. She sent a text to her three sisters, asking if they wanted to get together for a game night. Indigo had been the only one free and had decided that instead of playing games they needed a girl-talk session and plenty of cocktails.

The cocktails sounded like a great idea. The girl talk? Sage wasn't so sure. But she'd be happy to listen to whatever her sister wanted to talk about. "So, how are things at work?" Sage asked her as they walked across the parking lot toward the Troll Bridge. "Is that new guy still flirting with you?"

Indigo slipped her arm through her sister's and laughed softly. "Every chance he gets. I'm telling you, if he wasn't my employee, I'd have already helped him out of those low riding jeans."

"Really?" Sage asked her, knowing that although her sister

talked a big game, she wasn't really one for casual sex. She tended to require a deeper connection before she was interested in getting intimate with anyone. "It's like that?"

Indigo paused for just a moment. Her hands were on her waist, and she tapped her fingers on her belt like she always did when she was contemplating something. Finally she shook her head once and then kept walking.

"Care to share what you were just thinking?" Sage prompted as she hurried to catch up to her.

"Sure. I was thinking over what you asked, trying to decide if things really were like that. I didn't like the answer, so I chose to ignore your question." She shrugged one shoulder, making her asymmetrical blouse slide down her arm on the right side, showing her entire shoulder.

"That looks good like that," Sage said, gesturing to the shirt. "Wear it like that from now on. Wear it like that again when you finally agree to that date with Mr. Flirty. Because we both know that if you're interested like that, then no amount of fighting it is going to stop you."

"I'm not going to date him. It's inappropriate," Indigo insisted.

"Sure, you're not. What if he quits and finds a new job?"

"He's not going to do that," she said, sounding a little down. "And we both know I'm not going to leave. I love it too much. So we're destined to just be work spouses."

"We'll see," Sage said then tossed her head back, laughing.

"Very funny," her sister said, her tone very dry. "And what about you and August West? Are you going to get friendly with him south of the border?"

"What?" Sage asked, confused. "Are you asking if we're headed to Mexico, because—"

"No. Oh my gods." Indigo laughed so hard that tears

streamed down her cheeks. "No. Dense much? She glanced down her body and stared pointedly at her crotch. "South of the border. You know, below the belt? I'm asking if you're considering ripping his pants off him."

"I hadn't really thought about it," Sage started. "We're not... I mean, it's not anything serious. We're just friends and—" Her gaze landed on an all too familiar dark-haired man who'd just wrapped his arm around an attractive guy who was looking up at him adoringly.

"Sage?" her sister asked.

But Sage was too busy watching August kiss the man on the temple. Shock was radiating through her limbs, rendering her temporarily paralyzed.

"What's going on?" Indigo must've finally noticed August because she blew out a breath and said, "Oh."

Sage suddenly turned to her sister. "Did you know?"

"Know what?" Indigo frowned at her. "That he had a boyfriend? Obviously not. I would've said something."

"He's gay?" Sage muttered under her breath.

"Or bi. Or some other distinction from the LGBTQ+ alphabet," Indigo said.

Sage finally tore her gaze from the man she'd been crushing hard on for the last three days and blurted, "Why does this keep happening to me?"

Indigo raised both eyebrows, looking stunned. "You mean you've been blown off so your date could go out with another man more than once?"

"What? No. Not that I'm aware of," Sage said, blinking at her sister.

"Then what are you talking about? What keeps happening to you?"

"Life. Bullshit. You know, every time I start to like someone or think my life is going smoothly, I get a freakin' curve ball. What did I do to piss off the goddess, huh?"

"Okay, maybe hanging out in the same place as August isn't a great idea," Indigo said, turning and steering her back toward the parking lot.

Sage planted her feet and braced herself as Indigo tried to tug her along toward the car. "I'm not leaving."

Her sister turned around and looked at her. "You don't need to prove anything to anyone Sage. We can go to another pub. It's no big deal."

"No, I'm not letting him run me off. The Troll Bridge has my favorite drink. And I'm not leaving until I get it."

Indigo's lips twitched and Sage knew she had her.

"Come on. You know you want that blackberry lemon martini. No one else in town has anything like it. So unless you want to drink the latest local brewery's lager all night, I suggest we go in there and ignore the jackass who stood me up."

"If you're sure," Indigo said.

"I'm sure." Sage turned around and marched right into the pub. At first, she didn't see August or his date, and she started to wonder if they'd left already. But then a couple moved away from the window, and she spotted them sitting out on the patio with Levi Kelley and Silas Ansell. *Isn't that sweet,* she thought with a heavy amount of sarcasm. Boys' night. He could have just told her instead of saying something came up. What was it? A phone call from his date? She scowled and plopped down on a stool at the bar.

Indigo leaned forward and waved the bartender down. Just a few moments later, she handed Sage a purple drink and clinked their glasses together in a toast. "To not giving a shit," Indigo said.

Sage chuckled and then downed the drink in four long

gulps. She set the glass back down, eyed the bartender, and said, "Another, please."

His lips twitched with amusement. "It's been that kind of night, has it?"

"That kind of month. Keep em coming, will you?"

The handsome bartender with the dragon tattoo covering one arm nodded. "You got it."

"I'm going to date him," Sage told her sister as she jabbed her thumb in the bartender's direction.

"Does he know that?" Indigo asked, looking over the rim of her glass at her sister.

"Nope. But he'll figure it out when I'm in his car and we're headed to dinner." She gave Mr. Dragon tattoo a grin and watched while he made her another drink. When he put it in front of her, she asked, "Italian or French?"

"Italian or French what? Wine?" he asked.

"No. Food. Which do you prefer?"

"Oh, that's easy. Italian every day of the week. Though I won't pass up a great butter and wine sauce. Are you looking for a recommendation on where to eat?"

"No," she said with a soft chuckle. "I'm looking for a date."

"Oh." His eyes lit with understanding, but then he frowned. "If I was single, I'd love to volunteer, but since I'm not, I'm going to have to pass. Thank you though. It would've been my pleasure to take out one of the Easton girls."

"Hot, charming, *and* faithful," Indigo said with a sigh. "The very least you could have done was be a jackass when you turned her down so that we could trash talk you all night." She winked at him and then held her almost empty glass up. "Don't let me see the bottom of this tonight, okay?"

"You've got it," the bartender said, looking amused at her antics.

Sage swiveled until she was facing her sister. "How do you do that?"

"Do what?"

"Flirt so effortlessly," Sage said, exasperated. Why did that come so easily to Indigo and Lily and seem to elude Sage so completely? She swore she looked and sounded like a fool when she tried to be flirty. The only way she seemed to be able to get a guy's attention was by letting it all hang out while she was literally hanging from the window of her own vehicle. Yeah, that hadn't been ten kinds of embarrassing or anything. No wonder August had stood her up for that incredibly beautiful man sitting next to him. Hell, Sage didn't even blame him. She might've made the same choice if she were him.

No, she wouldn't have.

Sage would have kept her commitment. She'd never cancel on anyone last minute just because someone hotter and sexier asked her out. She sipped her drink as she continued to watch August and his date. When the other man leaned in, tucking his face against August's collar, Sage wondered how long it'd be before they were leaving together.

She was about three—or was it four—drinks in when her vision began to swim. Her sister was talking to her, saying something about creating a dating profile, but Sage didn't want to do that. She'd already found the guy she wanted to date. Too bad he'd found one, too.

"Dammit." She slammed her drink down on the bar and jumped up. Immediately she stumbled, nearly falling on her ample backside before she steadied herself.

"Whoa. Where are you going?" Indigo asked, trying and failing to grab Sage's hand.

"To do what... um, I should've done the moment we walked in here." She heard herself slurring her words. *Slurring*. She was *slurring* words. Sage Easton never drank enough for it to affect her speech patterns. Surely it wasn't as bad as she thought. It was just loud in the pub, and the noise was affecting her hearing. That must be it.

She moved toward August, his date, and the two superstars. Normally she never bothered celebrities. Sage tried to be as respectful as possible so that they didn't feel like they were getting gawked at. It's why most of them chose Befana Bay in the first place.

But tonight, they were on a double date with August. And he deserved every bit of the wrath she planned to unleash on him. Sage, although wobbly, did manage to make it through the pub's main floor and was just about to reach the patio when a chair jumped out in front of her and nearly took her out. She stumbled, grabbed onto the shirt of a guy who was brushing past her, and righted herself without ending up flat out on the floor.

"Whoa, hey, are you all right?" a woman who was vaguely familiar asked her. She had red hair, bright blue eyes, and flawless skin.

Sage reached out and caressed her cheek. "I'm going to need your skincare routine. Just lovely."

The woman carefully removed her hand and said, "Ask me when you have a chance of remembering."

"I'll remember," Sage said, tapping her temple. "I remember everything."

"Sure, you do." The woman was laughing when Sage stumbled out onto the patio. She had to take a moment to orient herself before she spotted August again.

There he was. Just sitting there way too close to his date. Though he didn't have his arm around him anymore. That was something. Except the too-handsome-for-his-own-good date was leaning into him and resting his head on August's shoulder.

Sage marched up to them and said, "Excuse me, sir. But I'm the one who is supposed to be sitting there."

The handsome man blinked up at her. "I'm sorry, what?"

She waved a hand at him and narrowed her eyes. "August is my date. I think it's time for you to get up so that he can buy me that drink he owes me."

"Sage?" August said, rising to his feet. "What's going on?"

"What's going on?" she scoffed. "I think I'm the one who's supposed to be asking you that question." She turned to Levi and Silas. "Can you believe him? He canceled our date because he said something came up. And here he is, with this guy." She waved frantically at the man who'd been snuggling August just moments ago. "Something came up all right. Someone better. Someone far prettier than me. But couldn't he have at least gone someplace outside of town so I wouldn't have to see or hear about it?"

The pretty man stood too. "I'm sorry. I didn't mean to mess up anyone's evening. I should go."

August reached out and grabbed his wrist before he could leave. "You didn't mess anything up, Nathan. This is all just a misunderstanding."

"It sure is," Sage said, snapping her fingers as if she'd just made some brilliant point. "A misunderstanding on my part. Here I was thinking you actually wanted to date me, but instead, you're dating him. I think you must be dating your roommate too. That's why all her clothes are in your closet."

"You're dating Kelly?" Silas asked August, surprise evident in his face. "Since when?"

"I'm not dating Kelly. For the love of the goddess. I have

never dated Kelly and I never would. He's… like my brother. Family."

"He?" Sage asked. "Your roommate's a he? Damn, I'm an idiot." She bopped herself in the head with her palm. "So you *are* gay," she said flatly.

"Holy hell," August muttered while Silas and Levi barely held in their laughter. Nathan looked like a deer caught in headlights.

August hurried over to Sage's side. "Come on, boozy Sage. It's time to go."

"Just answer me this one thing," she demanded. "All those clothes in your closet. Do they really belong to Kelly, or do you have a girlfriend on the side?"

He rolled his eyes. "Kelly's a drag queen, Sage. He's out on tour right now. And the reason half his clothes are in my closet is because he needed the space and I had it. Just like I told you before. End of story. Now let's go before this little scene makes the Befana Bay gossip column."

As August was dragging her away, she suddenly had a terrible feeling that she'd offended someone. "Wait!" She planted her feet and turned back to the table, confused as to why she saw amused faces. "I don't have anything against gay people. I swear. I just…" She waved helplessly at August. "I'd be just as angry if he'd been out with a woman."

Levi reached out and squeezed her hand. "We know, Sage. Don't worry about it. We understand."

"You do?" she asked, feeling like a weight had been lifted off her shoulders.

"Sure," Silas said, his eyes glinting with humor. "Who wouldn't want Mr. Tall, Dark, and Helpful all to themselves for a night?" Silas blew her a kiss. "Now try not to say anything else until you sober up. You'll thank yourself for it."

"I'm not drunk," she called out to them.

Silas and Levi cracked up while Nathan cracked a tiny smile.

"I'm not, you know," she said to August as soon as they got outside.

"Not what? A pain in my ass?"

"Mad that you date guys," she said with a hiccup.

He let out a heavy sigh. "Not that it matters, but I don't actually date guys, Sage. I date women."

"But I saw you kiss that guy," she said, frowning. She had seen that, right? It wasn't a hallucination?

"You probably did, but now isn't the time for explanations. Let's get you home so you can sleep this off."

"You don't have to take me. My sister is here. She'll drive me."

"You mean the one who crawled into the back seat of her car and fell asleep?" he said, peering into the back window of the vehicle.

Sage knocked on the window. "Hey, Indigo!"

Her sister didn't stir.

"Hey!" she tried again. "You have to let us in the car."

Indigo shifted slightly, and Sage heard the snick of the power locks unlocking. She walked over to the passenger side, climbed in, and glanced back at her sister. "You okay?"

"Yes," she said but didn't sit up. "Too much booze, not enough food. Now I have a stomachache."

"Don't worry, Indigo," August said. "I'll get you home."

"Blessed be," she mumbled.

Sage rested her head against the cool glass window and faded in and out of consciousness. Images of her making a fool of herself back at the bar kept flashing in her mind, but she couldn't quite hold on to them and wasn't one hundred percent convinced they were real. It didn't matter. If she didn't get out of the vehicle soon, she was likely to die from nausea before the alcohol poisoning took her.

Before she knew it, they were parked and August was standing at her door, taking her hand in his. "Come on, sleeping beauty. It's time to get into the house."

She glanced up, finding that they were parked in front of her house and her sister was gone. "Where's indigo?"

"We took her home already." He waggled his fingers, waiting for her hand.

Sage grabbed on and let him help her so that she didn't stumble. However, her legs had turned to jelly, and the first step she took rewarded her with a near faceplant. "Son of a jackhole!"

Her arms flew out to stop her from cracking her skull on the sidewalk, but before she hit the ground, August's strong arms were around her. And instead of planting her back on her feet, he just scooped her up into his arms and carried her to the front door.

"Do you have your keys on you?" he asked.

"I'm not sure." She tried to reach into her pocket, but for some reason didn't think her keys were there.

"Never mind." He set her down onto her feet and then gently coaxed her to sit on the porch swing. Once she was safely seated, she watched him rummage around her porch statues, find her hide-a-key, and get her door open. Then he was back, pulling her into his arms and carrying her across her threshold.

Sage clung to him, taking in the faint whiff of forest on his skin. Was that really the forest or some sort of scent? She figured with a guy like August, it had to be the real forest. What she wouldn't give to get lost with him for a few hours.

August strode through her house and straight into her bedroom as if he'd been there dozens of times in the past. *Only in my dreams*, Sage mused to herself.

"What dreams?" he asked, glancing down at her as he set her on her bed.

"Did I say that bit about dreams out loud?" she asked, giggling nervously.

His lips curved into that slow, sexy smile that Sage just knew she'd never be able to resist. She reached up and pressed her palm to his cheek. "I wanted to be the one you were kissing tonight."

"I know," he said.

"Cocky bastard," she said without any heat.

He chuckled. "If it makes you feel better, you're the one I wanted to be kissing."

"If that were true, you wouldn't have canceled on me and taken that pretty boy out instead."

"First off, I didn't cancel to take him out. I really did have something come up. I'll tell you about it when you're sober. And second, that wasn't a date. It was—"

"A booty call?" she answered for him.

"No, Sage. For the love of the goddess. I wasn't going to hook up with him. I was helping him out of a shitty situation. Maybe when you're ready to hear it, I'll explain. For now, why don't you tell me where you keep your painkillers? You're gonna need some if you don't want to wake up with an exploding head."

She pointed to her bathroom and watched as he retrieved the ibuprofen. And before she could ask for it, he produced a bottle of water, too. She took the provisions and looked up at him. "Thank you."

"You're welcome. Now take those and get some rest. I'm

going to take off. Call me when you wake up so I'll know you're okay."

"August?" she called after him.

He paused and looked back at her. "Yeah?"

"Will you stay with me tonight?" She wasn't sure why she was asking. It wasn't as if she was drunk enough that she needed to be watched through the night, not now anyway. She just had a feeling that he needed to stay.

"Here? With you?"

She nodded. "Just to sleep. Nothing else. I promise I don't snore."

"I wouldn't mind if you did," he said, still hesitating near her door. But she saw it in his expression when he made his decision to stay. All of the hesitation just drained out of him, and he stepped back into the room, closing the door behind him. "Mind if I strip out of these clothes?"

Her mouth went dry as she shook her head. "No," she said thickly. "Make yourself at home."

He laughed. "You don't know what you're offering." Then he winked and started to strip out of his clothes.

Afraid she'd make a fool out of herself watching him, Sage scrambled off the bed and hurried into the bathroom to brush her teeth and wash her face. By the time she reemerged, August had slipped into the bed and was sitting up against the headboard, his bare chest a marvel in male physique.

She cleared her throat while silently cursing herself for forgetting to take her pajamas with her into the bathroom. With her pajamas in her hand, she glanced at the bathroom door and then back at August, trying to decide whether she should just change in front of him or disappear back into the bathroom.

He seemed to catch on to her dilemma and took matters

into his own hands. Throwing the covers back, he climbed out of bed, wearing only a pair of royal blue boxer briefs.

Sage stared, unable to look away. He was just that beautiful.

"Get changed, Sage. I'm going to brush my teeth and use the head. Got an extra toothbrush?"

She nodded, still dumbfounded by those abs. "Under the sink."

"Thanks."

As soon as he closed the bathroom door, she hastily changed into her favorite moose print pajamas. She was lying with her head propped up on her pillows when he appeared in her bedroom again, looking every bit like sex on a stick. She couldn't help just imagining what it would be like to taste every single one of his abs.

"Stop staring at me like that," he said as he climbed back into the bed and laid down.

"Like what?" she asked.

"Like you're going to rip my boxers off the moment you get the chance."

She couldn't promise she wouldn't. The man just did it for her.

"Come here," he said, opening his arms wide for her to join him. "Get into bed. It's time to sleep."

"Just sleep, right? Nothing else?"

"Nothing else," he promised, pulling her into his arms and curling up around her.

Sage let out a contented sigh and snuggled into him, feeling like everything was finally right in her world.

CHAPTER 19

SOMEONE WAS POUNDING on Sage's skull from the inside of her head. She let out a groan and rolled over. Instantly, she knew that was a mistake when her stomach roiled and a wave of nausea washed over her. She froze, waiting for the queasiness to pass before she tried opening her eyes. When she was fairly certain she wasn't going to lose the contents of her stomach, she blinked her eyes open to the inky predawn light and was grateful to find that she was in her own bed.

Flashes of the night before started to infiltrate her cobwebby brain. Purple fruity drinks with Indigo. Flirting with the bartender. More purple drinks. Food? Had they eaten anything?

Her stomach rebelled at the thought of food, and she pressed her hand to her belly as she quickly pushed the idea from her mind.

August. He was there last night.

She hadn't been able to keep her eyes off him.

And then she'd— Oh no! Sage sat straight up in bed and instantly regretted it as her skin turned clammy and sweat broke out on her neck. "If I'm going to die, just take me out," she said as she eyed the ceiling, praying for someone, *anyone*, to put her out of her misery.

"I'd rather you lived," a groggy voice said from beside her.

Sage jumped right out of the bed, her heart pounding against her ribcage. The nausea had vanished, replaced by a rush of adrenaline as she stared open-mouthed at August. "How did you... I mean why are you..." She trailed off, vaguely recalling that she'd begged him to stay. "Never mind. I'm just gonna go lock myself in the bathroom and pretend none of this ever happened."

August chuckled softly as he climbed out of the bed and, to her disappointment, pulled his clothes on. Once he was dressed, he turned to her. "I'll give you a few minutes to collect yourself. Meanwhile, I'll be downstairs working on finding you some good hangover food."

"Don't say that word." She grimaced, wishing with everything she had that she could have a do-over in life.

He just grinned at her. "Hangovers are the worst. Don't worry, give me about thirty minutes and you'll be as good as new."

"Doubtful," she said, running a hand through her tangled hair. When her fingers got caught on a knot, she wished the earth would just open up and take her right then and there. Had she really just woken up next to August West, hungover and looking like a bird had taken up residence in her hair? That was it. She was done with whatever this was between them. There was no coming back from this humiliation.

But as she stood there, waiting for August to leave her bedroom, she was completely dumbstruck when he stopped next to her and pressed the softest kiss to her lips. "Um, what was that for?"

"Can't a guy kiss the woman he just spent the night curled up next to without having to explain himself?" he asked, his tone teasing.

She rolled her eyes and immediately regretted it. That was not a good idea.

He was still chuckling as he left the room.

Sage stared at the door for a long moment and then grudgingly hauled herself into her en suite bathroom. Once she looked in the mirror and spotted the makeup smeared under her eyes, her rat's nest hair, and the red lines from the wrinkled sheets on her face, she knew then and there she wouldn't ever have to worry about August West again. Because once she got out of the shower, dressed, and headed downstairs, she had no doubt that the man would have already run for the hills.

AUGUST WOKE up in a better mood than he had in ages. Hearing the soft sound of Sage breathing right next to him had done something to him. Just being in her presence had brought him a sense of calm. The type of peace he hadn't felt since before his father had shown up and started siphoning magic out of the bay. What would his life be like if he were able to wake up next to her every day? It was a thought that brought a smile to his lips.

He'd been awake for a few minutes when Sage had started to rouse from sleep. It had been obvious she wasn't feeling one hundred percent, and while that could have been amusing, his first thoughts were ones of concern. He didn't relish the thought of her being in pain. Especially since he had a feeling he might have been the reason she'd consumed more than her share of vodka the night before.

All he was focused on this morning was making her a potion to ease her symptoms and getting some food in her. Well, that and how adorable she'd looked with her hair sticking out everywhere and sleep lines all over her face.

Even though he'd slept right next to her all night, somehow waking up with her this morning had been more intimate. Seeing her raw, without her usual emotional armor, was a rare treat he wouldn't soon forget.

While the coffee was brewing, he found the downstairs bathroom, washed up, and did his best to clean his teeth with a spare tube of toothpaste and his finger. Once he was feeling human again, he went back to the kitchen to get their day started.

He'd just finished making pancakes when Sage appeared in the kitchen doorway. She was freshly showered with soft, natural makeup, and her hair had been washed and dried and was now piled up on the top of her head in a tidy bun. Her faded blue jeans were ripped in the knees and paired with an oversized T-shirt that hung off one shoulder. She looked both comfortable and like the sexiest woman he'd ever seen all at once. He let his gaze roam over her, taking in every detail before he met her eyes and said, "Good morning."

She crossed her arms over her chest and leaned against the doorframe. "Honestly, I've had better."

"I bet." He gave her a sympathetic smile and grabbed the glass of juice and herbs he'd compiled for her. "Drink this. You'll thank me after."

Sage eyed the glass but then shook her head. "I'm not sure my stomach can handle anything but crackers at the moment."

August, still holding the glass, walked over to her and placed it in her hand. "Just trust me on this one, will you?"

"You don't know what you're asking," she said with a grimace as her face turned a very pale shade of green.

"Oh, I do. I've been in your shoes a couple times. This concoction is the only thing that saved me."

"Okay, but when purple vomit ends up all over this floor, you're cleaning it up." Without waiting for his response, she squeezed her eyes shut and downed half the contents of the glass.

August watched as her face went from very pale green to a shade that resembled his grandmother's pea soup, and he took a step back, worried that she'd been right and purple vomit was about to cover every inch of the floor. But just as quickly, her color returned to normal, and she stared at the concoction in wonderment.

"What is in this?" she asked him before downing the rest of the potion.

"Mostly fresh-squeezed juice and natural herbs," he said.

She gave him an exasperated look as she walked over to her sink and deposited the glass. "Seriously? Fresh juice and herbs? Is the recipe some ancient family secret or something?"

He laughed. "No. The main ingredients are ginger and chamomile. I'll write it down for you, but it also requires some magic when you're mixing it all together."

She pursed her lips, studying him. "I thought your only magical ability was to talk to animals. Do you have an affinity for herbs, too?"

"Not really." He shook his head and produced a pocketknife that had a sapphire embedded on the top of the handle. "I use this when I need a magic boost." The sapphire glowed with magic, much in the same way that her glass pieces did that she sold in her shop.

"That's super handy," she said, her eyes fixated on the knife.

"It is. My mother got this for me when I turned thirteen. She said it was time I had access to the magic that other witches did.'" He shrugged his shoulder, realizing that he almost never showed anyone his knife. It was one of the very few things he had from his mother that made him feel connected to her. He kept it on his person at all times. "I don't use it often. Mostly just for things like potions or maybe when I need to coax a sticky lock. That kind of thing. It's not like it holds a lot of power."

"Can I?" She held her hand out, asking to hold it.

He hesitated for just a moment. For some reason, he didn't want to let it go. Not even for a few minutes.

"Sorry." She dropped her hand. "I didn't mean to be presumptuous."

"No," he said, feeling like a heel. "It's fine." He handed her his knife and shoved his hands into his pockets while he watched her inspect it.

Sage ran her fingers over the handle's inlay and then moved on to the sapphire. The stone lit up with magic, pulsing as if waiting for a command. "Wow. This is so unique. Do you know where your mom got this?"

He shook his head. "I'm pretty sure it's custom made. The magic in it is hers."

She took a few more seconds to admire the knife before she handed it back to him. "That's really special, August. I can see why you keep it to yourself. Thank you for showing me."

"Sure." He tucked it back into his pocket, comforted by the familiar magic that radiated through the fabric and warmed his skin.

"So, breakfast?" she asked, her eyes landing on the stack of pancakes.

"You really are feeling better," August said with a laugh. "You get the coffee, and I'll take care of the rest."

"You have a deal."

With coffee mugs and full plates of pancakes on the table, they sat across from each other and August waited while Sage dug in with gusto. With the first bite, her eyes rolled to the back of her head, and she let out the sexiest little moan. August decided he'd make her pancakes every day of his life if he could just be blessed with that sound.

"Oh my goodness, August," she gushed after a few bites. "What exactly did you put in this batter? These are the best damned pancakes I've ever tasted."

"You know, the usual. Vanilla, nutmeg, some other secret spices," he said with a smug smile.

"This again? You're really not going to tell me?" she asked with a huff of impatience.

"No way. I can't give up all my secrets. If you want these pancakes again, you'll just have to make sure I'm here for breakfast."

Her eyebrows rose halfway up her forehead. "This is all a ploy to get invited for a sleepover again? Please tell me you're joking."

August dropped his fork, placed his elbows on the table, and leaned toward her. "Why would I be joking?"

"After last night? The scene I caused? And then you had to take care of me." She scrunched her face up and glanced away. "No one wants to deal with *that* girl."

"It wasn't that bad," he said, unable to keep his lips from twitching in amusement.

"Now I know you're lying. Everything about last night

might not be crystal clear, but I do remember yelling at you for canceling and going on a date with someone much hotter than me. And I can't even blame you. It's not like we're really dating or anything. You were just doing me a favor and—"

"Wait just a minute there, Sage," he said in all seriousness. "Let me start by saying that in no way do I consider Nathan to be hotter than you."

"Now you're just being nice," she muttered and poked at the pancakes she hadn't been able to get enough of just moments before.

"No, I'm not," he said with a laugh. "I suppose Nathan is a good-looking man, but I'm not attracted to him. Since you seem to have missed my signals, let me be crystal clear here. I'm attracted to *you*. Understand? And while yes, our dating antics were just for show in the beginning, I think you should know that I really would like to date you. Not just show you how to have a good time or make your grandmother think you're out there living life instead of working all the time. Real dates. Me and you. Maybe a little kissing here and there."

"Kissing, huh?" she asked, her lips finally curving into her smile that he liked so much.

"I want to say it might be kind of a deal breaker," he said with a tiny wink.

"All right, I can agree to that, but I have some conditions of my own."

He sat back, palms up, and said, "Okay, lay them on me."

"Absolutely no kissing other people. I don't want to walk into a pub and see a guy, or a girl, hanging all over you. If we're dating, then it's just you and me." She paused and then took a deep breath and continued. "And I think I'm going to need that explanation about last night. I think you said it wasn't what I thought. That I was reading the situation wrong. But I don't really see how it could be any different than what it obviously looked like."

"You won't see that again," he assured her and then explained exactly what happened. "I'm telling you, Sage, Walker was such a jackass. I just really wanted to put him in his place and get Nathan out of that situation. He's a good friend, and I was just trying to help him out."

"Okay," she said slowly. "That's actually a really kind thing to do. But why were you there at the pub to begin with?"

"I canceled because my dad called and wanted to meet. When I went to the designated spot, he stood me up. Afterward, I thought about calling you, but I was just too frustrated. I planned to go home, but Levi convinced me to have a drink with them. And the next thing I knew, I was pretending to be Nathan's date and watching you and your sister get sloshed. Gotta say, as much as I wish I hadn't hurt you, it wasn't the worst evening I've ever had."

She smirked and then sobered quickly. "Your dad, huh? Any idea what he wants?"

"No, but I have plenty of questions." He quickly caught her up to speed on his grandmother's apparition and her warning. "I think that message has to be about him, and I want to know what he's up to before he does something that can't be fixed."

Sage reached across the table and covered his hand with hers. "I'm so sorry, August. That's a lot to deal with. And here I was thinking that I had things to worry about."

He narrowed his eyes as he studied her. "Has anything notable happened in the past forty-eight hours that I haven't heard about yet?"

"You mean other than my impressive display of public drunkenness?" she asked with a laugh.

"Yeah. Other than that." He could sense that there was something else. Something that was bothering her.

"After our lunch at The Salt Circle, I met up with my sisters. No big deal, right?"

"Sure," he agreed, though when a bunch of witches got together, there was always the potential for trouble.

"We chatted with Gran and then decided to engage in a broomstick race over the bay."

August grimaced, already guessing where this was headed. "Please tell me you used a spelled broomstick intended for those without magic."

"That's the thing. I did, but while we were out flying over the bay, my magic came back full force, and I couldn't stop myself from letting loose. And…" She scrunched her nose up and glanced away.

"And what? Your magic backfired? Did anyone get hurt?" he asked urgently, suddenly worried. But no, that couldn't be true. She and her sister wouldn't have been living it up at a bar the next night if anything awful had happened. He really needed to get a grip on himself. *Not everything involving magic ends with a tragedy, August.*

"No, it didn't backfire. It just winked out. And by then I was leaning into it full on instead of letting the spell do the work. And well, the broom kicked me off, and I landed in the bay." She wrapped her arms around herself and shivered.

No doubt she was remembering just how icy that water was. "How did you get out? Did your sisters come for you?"

"They would have, but they didn't have to." She smiled softly at him. "One of your orcas rescued me and hauled me to shore."

August sat back in his chair, stunned. "Really? Was it Tokia?"

She shook her head. "It was one of the young males. But I got the impression that she sent him."

He got up, moved to her side of the table, and held his hand out to her. She took it and let him tug her out of her chair. When he put his arms around her, she smiled softly at him. "What's this all about?"

"The orcas gave you their seal of approval. Now I know I've made the right choice." He pressed both hands to her cheeks and kissed her thoroughly, claiming her as his own.

CHAPTER 20

SAGE PARKED at the curb in front of her grandmother's house, grateful to have a fully functioning vehicle again. After she and August finished their breakfast, they'd gone and picked up his SUV at the Troll Bridge, returned Indigo's car, and then August had dropped her off at Auto Alchemy to get her RAV4. Despite waking up feeling like she'd needed a head transplant, her day had turned out to be pretty spectacular so far.

She was on cloud nine as she walked up the path to her grandmother's house. Not only was she happy about her new relationship status, it also occurred to her that she was no longer lying to her grandmother about dating August. Not that she'd really felt bad about it before. Her grandmother had instigated the problem when she'd zapped Sage's magic. But Sage had forgiven her... for the most part.

It was hard to ignore the fact that ever since Sage's magic had gone missing, she'd certainly been living a fuller life and was grateful for it.

"Gran?" she called. "Where are you?"

Bethany Befana's voice floated down from upstairs. "Up

here." Her footsteps echoed through the house as she glided down the stairs, looking radiant in her deep burgundy witch dress and matching lace-up high-heeled shoes. Her long hair was flowing behind her, making her look like she was ready to take on the supernatural world.

"You look lovely today, Grandma," Sage said, meeting her at the bottom of the stairs. "Where are you headed?"

"A dinner party with a bunch of the founding families. You know how we like to pull out all the stops to impress each other." She grabbed Sage's hand and walked with her over to the parlor in the front of the house. As they sat on the couch, she turned to her granddaughter. "What brings you by today, love?"

"Two things," Sage said. "Did you really sign me up to model for that sculpting class tonight?"

Bethany blanched. "Oh dear. I did do that, didn't I? She looked pained as she stared Sage in the eyes. "I never should have done that. I can get you out of it. Just let me..." She fumbled with her phone as she searched for the right number. "Ah, there it is." She hit Call and waited, only to scowl a few seconds later. "It says her mailbox is full. I can't even tell her you're not coming." She stood and quickly tried again, but of course she got the same recording. "I'll stop on my way and straighten this out."

Her grandmother was agitated, something Sage didn't see very often. "Gran?"

"Yes?"

Sage tugged her down to sit next to her again. "What's going on? You're never like this."

"I messed up, Sage. Badly." She turned away, hiding her pained expression. "What I did to your magic was uncalled for. And now the modeling? I just... I owe you the biggest apology."

"That's…" Sage started and stopped, not sure what to say. Her grandmother had already told her that she'd been wrong to mess with her magic, but this was nothing short of a breakdown. She wasn't sure how to handle it.

"You don't have to say anything, love. I just hope you accept my apology. I'm very sorry for interfering in your life like that. And now look at what I've done. I've ruined your business and volunteered you for that damned sculpture class. Just because I think that would be fun, it doesn't give me the right to try to force that on you. Especially when it comes to something like showing your body in public. I've been told that consent is serious, and I've crossed some lines. I promise to do better."

Stunned, Sage sat back on the couch and tried to process what she was hearing. Bethany Befana almost never admitted she'd made a mistake. She was far too proud. "Okay, I have to ask. Who talked to you about this?"

"You don't know?" Bethany asked, looking confused.

A pit in her stomach formed, and Sage was starting to dread the answer. "Please don't tell me it was August."

"August?" Bethany frowned. "No. I haven't seen him since you two were smooching out in front of The Salt Circle the other day."

Ahh, so her grandmother had seen that. Sage had wondered. "If not August, then who?"

"It was Prim. She marched in here this morning and really laid into me. She said she saw the flyer that you'd be modeling for the class and knew that you'd never sign up to do it and demanded to know how that happened. When I told her, she went ballistic. Told me just how out of line I was and that if I didn't figure out how to get your magic working again, I'd regret it for the rest of my life. And you know what, Sage? She's right. I got so fixated on what *I* thought you should be doing that I wasn't really paying attention to what you wanted or needed. Can you forgive me?"

Sage took her grandmother's hand in both of hers, stared into her deep green eyes, and honestly said, "I already have."

The relief on her grandmother's face was enough to make Sage want to tell her to not worry about it. That it didn't matter. But that would be a lie. It *did* matter. But that didn't mean she didn't love her grandmother or that they couldn't get through this.

"I was really, really angry at you at first. I think we can both agree that I had every right to that emotion," Sage said.

"You did." Bethany pressed her fingertips under her eyes, catching a few tears that had fallen.

"And Prim is right about that class, though I can just tell them there's been a mistake. I'm sure the students will live if they have to sculpt someone with clothes on." Sage gave her grandmother a pointed stare. "But still, don't ever sign me up for anything that I haven't already explicitly agreed to. Understand? You know how much I hate disappointing people. I don't want to feel obligated to do something that I might not like. I'm thirty years old, Gran. I don't need you running my life."

Her grandmother raised one of her eyebrows just enough to question that statement.

"Stop. You're not helping your cause," Sage said.

Bethany chuckled. "Okay, go on."

"I think that's it," Sage said. "Except just one more thing."

"Is it about August? You two aren't really dating, are you?"

Sage felt her lips curl into a wide grin. "Actually, Gran, that's the one good thing that has come out of this. We *are* dating. It was just for show at first, but now…" She shrugged. "I really like him."

There was silence in the room until Bethany stood and pumped her fist in the air. "I knew it!"

"Knew what?" Sage asked through narrowed eyes.

"That you two were perfect for each other. Maybe my methods were questionable, but I think it's clear that I really do know what's best for my girls."

Sage shook her head as she got to her feet. "You should have stopped while you were ahead."

Bethany let out a bark of laughter as she grabbed Sage's hand, stopping her. When their eyes met, her grandmother gave her the softest look she'd ever seen on the older witch's face. "I have high hopes for this relationship, but just so you know, if it doesn't work out, I'm on your side, no matter what. If he doesn't treat you well, you let me know about it. He'll wish he'd never messed with an Easton girl."

"You're scary sometimes, you know that?" Sage said.

"It comes with the territory. No leader gets out of the job without some mud on their hands." She pressed a papery kiss to Sage's cheek. "Now go let down that sculpting class. I have a dinner to get to."

"Wait. You didn't even hear why I stopped by," Sage said, chuckling to herself. "Sit for a minute. I have something to tell you."

Bethany did as her granddaughter asked and listened as Sage told her about the warning August had gotten at his house the day before. "He wanted you to know just in case his father is planning to do something stupid to mess up the town's magic," Sage said.

"What exactly did his grandmother say?"

"Um, something about someone stealing something and history repeating itself. Oh, then she mentioned Phillip, August's dad."

Bethany nodded. "That sounds like a family matter to me. But I'll tell the coven and we'll keep an eye on the magical health of both the bay and the community. Sound good?"

"Yeah," Sage said, feeling relief. The fact that her grandmother didn't seem to be worried settled her. She didn't love the implications that whatever the warning was pertained to August's family though. She didn't want him to have to deal with his father, not after he'd all but abandoned his son.

"Thanks, Gran," Sage said, giving Bethany a hug. "I'll go disappoint some artists. You go outshine all those other witches. I'll see you on Thursday for tarot."

"I'm looking forward to it," Bethany said as she held the door open for her granddaughter.

Sage waved and then hurried off to the sculpting studio.

CHAPTER 21

"ARE you ready to go in and break the bad news?" August asked Sage. They were standing in front of the art studio, peering in at all the students who were waiting to see her naked.

"No," she said honestly. "I hate conflict. I should have told her as soon as I learned my grandmother signed me up for this."

He reached over and grabbed her hand in his. "I'll go in with you. Be your moral support."

She smiled up at him. "You're not too disappointed you're not going to be taking the class?" He'd tried to get a spot, but she'd been right when she told him the class was full. Apparently, the instructor was in high demand.

"No." He scanned her body, and when he met her gaze again, he said, "I feel strongly that the first time you show me your body, it should be on your terms, not because you feel bad for bailing on a modeling job you never wanted."

She squeezed his hand and pressed up on her tiptoes to give him a soft kiss on the lips. "I think I like you."

"I like you, too, Sage Easton. Now come on. Let's go crush some dreams."

She sucked in a sharp breath, squared her shoulders, and walked in.

"Ahh, there's our model!" the instructor called, beaming at her. "We're so glad you're here. We were starting to think we were getting stood up."

"Oh, well, uh, I have some bad news," Sage said. "I'm really sorry but—"

"No. No, no, no, no! Not again!" The instructor looked like her head was going to explode. "This is the third time our model has canceled on us. How are my students ever going to learn the human form if no one will strip for them?"

The students heard her, and they all started to talk at once. One of them stood and called out, "If I have to make one more apple, I'm going to hurl all over this table."

"That's a little dramatic," August said, his eyebrows raised in surprise.

"This is a requirement for some of them to graduate from their masters of art," the instructor said tersely. "Without it, some of them are going to scramble to find another class."

"Find another class?" Sage asked. "I thought this was just a community art class, not a masters class. No one told me that." She glanced at the students, hating that she was going to be making their lives more difficult. "I was under the impression this was just a regular sculpting class, one that just anyone can sign up for."

"Well, it isn't," the instructor said coldly. "This was their requirement to sculpt the classical form. So unless you know of someone willing to participate in this ancient artform, then I'm going to have to ask you to leave." She clapped her hands together to quiet the class. "You heard her, students. The class isn't happening tonight." She shot daggers at Sage. "I was under the impression that this model had been thoroughly vetted. My mistake. It won't happen again. Keep your emails open and I will let you know when we can get back on track."

The room erupted with chatter ranging from disappointment to downright anger as the students started packing up.

"Wait!" Sage called. "I'll do it."

"You will?" August whispered from behind her. "Sage—"

"It' for college credit, August," she said over her shoulder. "I can't let them down."

"But you don't want to do this. Did you change your mind?" he asked.

"No, I just don't want to be the reason someone doesn't graduate," she said, knowing that she was grimacing.

"If you're really in," the instructor said, "We need you to hurry up and change. There's a robe waiting for you in the bathroom."

Sage nodded and then stared at the bathroom. For some reason, she couldn't seem to make her feet move. He hands began to shake, and she knew that if she went through with this, it was likely she'd end up with a full-blown panic attack. She turned to August with wide eyes and shook her head ever so slightly. There was no way she could stand in front of all those students sky clad and not pass out.

"I'll do it," August said from behind her.

She spun around. "What?"

He turned to the instructor. "Does it matter if your model is male or female?"

Her face was bright with excitement, and Sage thought the woman might pass out at the idea of August baring his goods. "No, not at all. Are you saying you're modeling for us tonight?"

"That's what I'm saying. As long as Sage can have her own station to try sculpting. That's my deal, take it or leave it," he said.

"Oh, no problem," she said, sounding absolutely giddy. "I'll give her my station." She absentmindedly waved toward the station near the front of the room. "Sit there. If you lose any of my tools, you'll get a bill in the mail."

Sage stared at her, both amused and annoyed by the instructor's attitude. Then her gaze shifted to August, and she felt a rush of gratitude. He'd known she was anxious about modeling and had stepped in so that she didn't have to. Who did things like that?

August West. That's who. He might possibly be the best man she'd ever known.

He caught her eye and she mouthed, *Thank you.*

He gave her one of his famous winks and then followed the instructor to the bathroom so he could get ready to model.

Sage took her seat in the instructor's spot and ran her hands over the clay. Immediately she started to relax. It had been weeks since she'd made anything in her studio, and she was starting to feel it. A part of her *needed* to create, and without the ability to make her glass pieces, she'd started to feel as if she was missing a part of herself.

The clay was cool under her touch as she picked it up and started to wedge it against the table, working the ball so that it didn't contain any air bubbles while she was sculpting. She was so focused on her task that she didn't notice when August returned to the class. It wasn't until she heard the woman next to her suck in a sharp breath that she glanced up to find August standing in the middle of the room, wrapped in a robe that barely covered his backside.

She let her gaze roam down his legs, taking in his muscular

thighs, his calves, and then moving back up until she met his penetrating stare. He was looking right at her, his hands resting on the belt of the robe.

The instructor introduced him and rattled off some instructions. She said something about each of them having an hour to sculpt his torso and then they'd have to turn them in.

Sage ignored it all. Her eyes were locked on August, and her heart was pounding as if this were a defining moment in their relationship.

Then suddenly, it dawned on her that she was going to see him naked for the first time in front of over a dozen students.

August started to undo the belt of his robe. Sage couldn't keep her eyes off his hands. And the moment he went to drop the belt and open his robe, she jumped up.

"Nope. I can't do this." Sage hastily wiped off her hands and called, "I gotta go."

August called after her. "Sage, wait!"

She paused at the front door but didn't turn around. "Sorry, August. Text me when you're done. We'll... I dunno. Have dessert or something."

"Or something," one of the students said with a snicker.

Sage pushed the door open and stumbled out into the cool night air. She stood out on Witch Tower Road, taking deep breaths and trying not to think about what an idiot she'd just been. How old was she? Thirty? And she'd run from seeing a grown man naked. Had she suddenly teleported back to junior high? Feeling ridiculous, she hung her head and headed for her RAV4.

"Was it that bad?" August asked as he took a seat next to Sage at The Salt Circle's bar.

She glanced over at him. "Which part?"

He chuckled softly. "The part where you were almost forced to see me naked."

She took a long sip of her lemonade and then turned to him. "No. I just realized that I didn't want the first time I see you naked to be at an art class."

"I see," he said with a thoughtful nod. "So if the model had been anyone else but me, you'd have stayed?"

"Yes." She sipped her lemonade again. "Was it terrible?"

He shrugged. "Not really. Or at least it wasn't until one of the guys came up and started measuring my junk."

"You're not serious." She couldn't help herself when she glanced down at his crotch. When she looked up again, he was giving her a pointed look.

"Need a ruler for that inspection?" he deadpanned.

Sage groaned. "Sorry. I just had a visual and..." She waved a hand, indicating it was time to move on from that subject. "Never mind. I just really want to thank you for stepping in." She let out a humorless laugh. "And to apologize for running out."

August stood, took her hand in his, and gently tugged her off the stool. "You have absolutely nothing to apologize for. I'm actually pretty damned flattered that I mean enough for you to care that much."

Sage reached up and caressed his cheek. "You sort of snuck up on me, you know."

"I'm not sure I know what you mean, Sage," he said, leaning into her touch.

"This. You. Me. Whatever is going on between us. I know we just decided that we're dating, but you really took me by surprise. You and your easy, go-with-the-flow attitude. The guy who works to live instead of lives to work like I do. We don't make sense on paper."

"We really don't," he agreed.

"But here I am, hoping with everything I have that you'll take me home tonight." The words had just tumbled out. She hadn't meant to say them, but now that she had, she was glad. Because there wasn't anyone she'd ever wanted more than August West.

"Do you mean that?" he asked, searching her eyes as if they actually were the window to her soul.

"I mean it."

He nodded once, grabbed her hand, and said, "Let's go."

Sage held onto his hand with both of hers and followed him to his SUV. Without a word, he held the passenger door open for her. And once he was in the driver's seat, he didn't ask where she wanted to go. He just took her home.

His house was completely dark except for the porch light. Sage studied the house before climbing out of the vehicle. She knew without a doubt that she wanted to remember every detail of this night.

When they got inside, August turned to her and brushed a lock of hair out of her eyes. His lips twitched with a hint of a smile when he said, "Just because you almost saw mine, that doesn't mean you're obligated to show me yours."

"I know," she said, a wave of calm washing over her. She looked into his eyes and slowly tugged her shirt up, up, up, until she pulled it completely off, leaving her in only her favorite red-lace bra.

August's expression turned heated as he looked at her like he was going to devour her.

She made a show of licking her lips before turning and

heading toward the stairs to his bedroom. She felt the weight of his steps behind her, and just because she knew it would drive him insane, she paused at the base of the steps, made sure her back was to him, and then shed her bra, leaving her bare from her waistline up.

"Damn, Sage," he said softly from behind her. "This was worth the wait."

She tossed her hair over her shoulder as she looked back at him. "It had better be." Then she smiled and quickened her pace.

August matched her stride for stride, and when they were finally in his room, he kicked the door shut and grabbed her by the waist, finally getting a handful of all that smooth skin. "You're gorgeous, Sage."

"So are you," she said, running her hands under his T-shirt, over his abs, and then his pecs.

He reached back, grabbed a handful of his T-shirt, and roughly pulled it off.

"That's better," she said softly as she stepped closer, pressing her lips to his. "But I still haven't had a chance to measure your junk."

He chuckled. "I hope you brought your ruler."

She held up her hand, glanced at it, and then back down to the obvious bulge in his jeans. "I think I'll manage."

Then, as her hands got to work, freeing him of his jeans, he leaned against the wall, reveling in her touch. But when she had him completely naked and was eyeing every spare inch of him, he couldn't take it anymore. He returned the favor, divesting her of her jeans and underwear, leaving her bare and perfect before him.

August, already about to lose his mind, claimed her mouth so thoroughly that when he finally pulled back from the kiss,

Sage was breathless and a little unsteady on her feet. He ran his hands down her sides, along her hips, and when they found her bare butt cheeks, he lifted her up and took her over to the bed. He gently laid her down, crawled over the top of her, and said, "Tell me now, Sage. Do you want this? Do you want me?"

"I want you. I want *all* of you," she said in a husky voice. "Now stop talking and give me what I need."

"I hope you cleared your schedule, because this is going to take all night," he said.

Sage grinned at him and said, "Thank the goddess."

CHAPTER 22

AUGUST CURLED UP NEXT to Sage's body and lightly kissed the back of her neck. The harvest moon was shining in through the window, giving him enough light to make out all of her soft curves. In an hour or so, the sun would start to come up, and he just prayed that the magic of this night wouldn't vanish with the cloak of darkness.

"Hmm, that's nice," she said sleepily.

"I can be nicer." He ran a hand down her side, reveling in their closeness.

She stretched and purred like a cat. "You've been plenty nice. Give a girl a chance to recover a little, okay?"

He chuckled. "I can be patient."

Sage rolled over, smiling into his eyes. "Yes, yes you can." She pressed her fingertips to his chest, taking her time exploring him again. "Can I ask you something?"

He caught her hand and brought her fingers up to his lips, kissing them. "Sure. Anything."

"You have a lot of really cool artwork in your house. The paintings of the town downstairs and the mosaic in here. I've never seen them before. Where did you get them, and why isn't the artist showing them at the art gallery or at least the monthly art market?"

"That's what you want to talk about right now? When you have a naked man next to you?" he asked, trying to sound offended, but failing when he let out a small laugh.

"I'm an artist, remember? This is just foreplay for me." She leaned in and nipped lightly at his neck, sending a shiver down his spine.

"If you keep doing that, there's not going to be any talking," he warned.

"I think we can multitask." But instead of continuing her sweet assault on his neck, she laid back on her pillow and looked up at him expectantly.

He wanted to roll her over, cover her body with his, and make her his for the third time that night, but he knew he needed to give his body some time to recover. So instead, he let his hands roam, doing his best to memorize every curve. "I'd say you know the artist very well. In fact, you now know him intimately. And if you give him a few minutes, you'll find out just how much stamina he has too."

Sage blinked up at him, her eyes shining with recognition in the moonlight. "August, are you saying you paint?" There was excitement in her tone as she pressed up on one elbow and looked down at him. "What about the mosaic? Was that you, too?"

"Yep. Both me." He grinned up at her, pleased he'd been able to surprise her. "Is it so unbelievable that I could be decent with a paintbrush?" he teased.

"No. Not at all." Her face was serious now. "But it *is* unbelievable that you don't have a gallery dedicated to your work.

It's so good, August. You could make a living just selling your art. And that glass mosaic? I gotta say that if I didn't have any morals, I'd have already ripped it off your wall and run away with it."

"If you did that, then you wouldn't ever learn just how much stamina I have." He'd always been a little uncomfortable talking about his art. It was just easier to deflect. How could he explain what his art meant to him and why he'd never been interested in selling it?

"August, I'm serious. You could make a killing." She sat up, and he could see her business mind take over. "Even if the gallery is too full, I'd put your work in my studio in a heartbeat. I mean, the mosaics would be a no-brainer. We could have an event, call it something like, The Heart of Befana Bay. Because your work is so heavily focused on your love of this town. We'd get it catered and maybe get some entertainment. Really go all out to introduce your art to the town and—"

"Sage," he said firmly as he sat up and faced her. "Stop."

She clamped her mouth closed and shook her head. "Sorry. I got a little carried away there, didn't I?"

"A little?" He didn't bother to hide his annoyance.

"Sorry." She grimaced, obviously realizing she'd way overstepped. "You don't want any of that, do you?"

He shook his head. "No. I make art for me. Or for my friends. Like that painting of Silas and Levi." He gestured to the painting sitting by his door. "It's a gift I'll give to them when they go back to Keating Hollow. I do it to relax. I don't *want* to turn it into a job. I'm not interested in that. I'd rather just make what I want, when I want, even if it just piles up in my garage. I don't want to do production or feel like I need to make popular items. That would ruin it for me."

She bit down on her bottom lip, and he could tell that she wanted to say something but didn't think she should.

He let out a sigh. "Just say it."

"Do you have stockpiled up in your garage?"

He groaned. Why had he mentioned that? A voice in the back of his mind whispered, *Because it bothers you that it's just sitting there.* But the idea of turning his art into a business made him queasy. "Yes. But the best ones are hanging on my walls."

She snuggled back into her pillow and placed a hand lightly on his chest. "Believe it or not, I do understand how you feel."

A bark of laughter erupted from his lips. "I don't believe that. Not you. Your entire life is built around selling your art. You live for it even."

She shrugged. "Maybe. But creating is my happy place, and I sell it so that I can create every day. It's a tradeoff. Would I rather be making experimental pieces? Some days, yes. But a lot of days I just enjoy the rhythm and consistency of doing what I'm good at. It fulfills me. I'm sure it's different for everyone."

He didn't say anything to that. He wasn't sure what he should say. That his mother had always told him he'd be a famous artist someday? That he'd grown up thinking that was exactly the path he'd take? She had been so proud of him. Her dreams for him had been monumental. But when she died, those dreams seemed to have died with her. When he painted, it was like he painted just for her. Sharing that with the world, every day, all day, it was just too much.

"Hey," she said softly. "You okay?"

"Sure. I appreciate your thoughts on my art. I just don't think I'm ever going to be ready to sell it."

"I didn't mean to hit a nerve." She entwined her fingers

with his and gently squeezed. "I just got so excited and started carrying on as if it's any of my business. Forgive me?"

He looked down at the woman he knew he was falling for and shook his head slightly.

"No, you don't forgive me?"

"There's nothing to forgive," he said, pulling her closer so that their bodies were touching. "And to be honest, although this just started between us, I think that going forward, my business is going to be your business. Don't ever be afraid to tell me what you're thinking. I'm a big boy. I'll let you know if I don't agree."

She moved her leg so that it was entangled with his and said, "Okay. I like that." Her smile widened. "Then just one more thing and I'll drop this subject."

He groaned good naturedly. "All right. Let's hear it."

"If, and I do mean *if*, you ever decide to offer your work for sale, I'd be more than happy to handle that end of it. Either in my shop, or I can find galleries that are willing to take them on. I've been doing it for years, and not to toot my own horn too much, but I'm really good at it."

He frowned.

"Oh, come on. Stop looking at me like that," she demanded as she reached up and touched his lips. "It's just an offer. You don't have to do anything with it at all if you don't want to."

He bit down gently on her finger, and when she pulled it away, he said, "It's not that. I just wouldn't want you to take on more work. You work hard enough already."

The tension eased from her face as she relaxed again. "Is that all? Don't worry about that. Your work is the kind that sells itself. Trust me when I say it would be a pleasure. Now, no more talking. I'm ready to learn all about that stamina you've been telling me about."

"Finally," he said, rolling her over so that she was beneath him. "I hope you're ready for this because—"

The doorbell chimed, startling them both, and it was followed by a loud banging on the door and someone calling his name.

"What the hell? It's like five in the morning," August ground out as he rolled off Sage and started climbing out of the bed.

"Please tell me that isn't a jilted lover banging on your door," Sage said as she pulled up the sheet to cover herself.

He shook his head as he pulled on his clothes. "I don't have any jilted lovers."

"That's what they all say."

"I'll be right back," August said as he opened his door and glanced back at her and grinned. "Don't even think about leaving. We have unfinished business."

August didn't have any idea who'd show up at his house that early in the morning. Maybe his father, but the voice sounded female. Besides, his father would never make that kind of scene. His stepmother, maybe. If she couldn't get ahold of Phillip, Sissy might fly all the way to Washington and demand that August help her track him down. She was a little unhinged, just like his dad.

A variety of possibilities ran through his head on the way down the stairs, including some of Kelly's family, his ex, or even a crazy fan who was looking for August's famous cousin. But when he pulled the door open, he wasn't prepared to see his mother's best friend standing there looking frantic and like her world had been torn apart.

"Ophelia? What are you doing in Befana Bay?"

"I have to talk to you. It's important." She swept past him and into the house as if she'd done it numerous times before.

"You can't be here right now," August said, his heart racing. "I have company and—"

Then he heard footsteps on the stairs and froze.

"Sage," he started, not at all sure what he could say to salvage this situation.

"Ophelia Vincent?" Sage said from behind him, her voice shaking. "Is that really her?"

"Yes, it's me," the woman said, gazing at Sage with interest. She glanced at August. "You didn't tell me you two were dating."

"You didn't tell her we're dating?" Sage parroted, her voice on edge. "Does this mean you've been in contact with her all these years?"

"Yes, we have," Ophelia said calmly.

"I'm not talking to you!" Sage shouted and then whirled on August. "She killed my mother, August! What is she doing here?"

"I don't know—" he started and looked helplessly at the woman he'd thought of as a second mother his entire life.

Sage stared at August, her eyes bright with tears. Then she glanced at Ophelia and again back at August, obviously gutted. "I can't do this."

Before August could stop her, she was out the door and running down his driveway.

CHAPTER 23

SAGE TORE out of August's house with no thought about how she was going to get home. She only knew that she couldn't be in that house. Not with Ophelia Vincent there. She was the reason Sage's mother, Dahlia, had died when Sage was just a young girl.

People tried to say that it was just a love potion gone wrong, but everyone knew the truth. The love potion was an illegal one that Ophelia had started, and when it went wrong, Dahlia, who was skilled at herb magic, had tried to salvage it to save her friend. Only instead of it killing Ophelia, it had taken Dahlia instead.

Afterward, Ophelia had been questioned by the Magical Task Force and everyone expected that she'd be convicted of manslaughter at the very least, but they'd let her go and proclaimed it all an accident. The coven of Befana Bay had been livid. Sage had always wondered why her grandmother hadn't sued Ophelia. She imagined it was because the town had systematically ostracized her, and not long after she was cleared by the Magical Task Force, she'd left Befana Bay and had never come back.

Until now.

But why? And why was she at August's house in the middle of the night? Sage's head swam with all sorts of fantastical reasons ranging from they had some sort of romantic entanglement to dabbling in illegal magic.

But neither of those things seemed to make sense to Sage. Ophelia was at least thirty years August's senior. While she knew that didn't mean a romantic relationship was impossible, she just couldn't see it. And as for illegal magic, hadn't they just spent the past week trying to find and stop August's dad from causing further damage after he siphoned magic off Befana Bay?

No. He wasn't messing around with forbidden magic. August didn't even have the kind of magic that could be channeled into fantastical spells and curses. He only talked to animals. It was magic, but not the kind that was sought after by power-hungry witches.

Her head started to pound as she heard August calling her name. Was he following her? She couldn't talk to him right now. She had to get home and get her thoughts straight. Find a way to make her heart stop bleeding. She cut through the woods, heading for the shoreline, knowing that it would be a quicker path back to town.

But just before she burst through the trees, a flash of bright light came out of nowhere and blinded her. She instinctively threw her hands up, calling on her magic. Her fingers tingled, and she knew her magic had returned. She just wasn't sure where to aim it. Scanning the woods, she peered through the trees and saw nothing.

"August? Is that you?" she asked, feeling that anger building again. If he'd come after her and then somehow used magic to stop her, she was going to lose her mind.

There was no response.

"If that's you, I don't want to talk. Not now. Maybe not ever! Do you understand?"

A rustling of the trees sounded to her right and she spun. A woman dressed in a long black cloak, with auburn hair spilling out of the hood materialized right in front of her.

"What the hell!" Sage cried, backing up to put distance between her and the woman. "Did you come here with Ophelia?"

"No," the woman said, her voice icy. "But I imagine once she realizes we have you, we'll be seeing her shortly." The woman snapped her fingers and suddenly arms came around Sage from behind, trapping her.

Sage opened her mouth to scream, but before she could get any sound out, a rag was clasped over her mouth. She struggled, frantic to get free. But within seconds, her limbs went limp, and she was plunged into darkness.

SHE WAS LYING on something hard, and Sage's mind was full of cobwebs as she struggled to form a coherent thought. If she'd just wake out of her sleep coma and return to full consciousness, maybe her mind would start working again. The heavy blackness that had taken her started to fade, and the first thing she registered was that she had the worst case of cottonmouth she'd ever experienced. "What happened?" she grumbled, her head pounding and her stomach rolling. "How much did I drink last night?"

"You weren't drunk. You were drugged," a male voice rasped.

Sage's eyes flew open, and she bolted upright, blinking rapidly to try to clear her blurry eyes. "Where am I?"

"Crystal Point Island," the man said.

"Why?" She peered at the man who was chained to the stone wall across from her, and that's when everything came into focus. The man wasn't just any man. He was August's father. And they were in some sort of cave that was lit with open-fire torches. Water dripped down in a steady rhythm from somewhere near the back of the cave. "Phillip?" she managed to say as she frantically tried to free herself from her shackles.

There was no give to her restraints, and it quickly became clear to her that she wasn't getting free anytime soon. Not unless... She closed her eyes and concentrated on calling her magic. It tingled at the tips of her fingers, and she let out a sigh of relief.

"It won't work," Phillip said from across the cave.

She ignored him, and instead thought of her grandmother and her sisters, imagining that they were there with her, sending her their strength. Magic rushed through her limbs with an intensity that stole her breath, but when she unleashed it onto the shackles, intending to break them apart, nothing happened.

At all.

The magic just seemed to seep into the steel as if she were feeding it magic instead of trying to destroy it. "What the hell?" Determined to get free, she tried again. This time her magic pulsed so strongly that her vision blurred with the effort, and when she let it go, she called, "Destroy these chains that bind!"

The magic burst from her in a brilliant display of light and then just fizzled as if a bucket of water had been thrown onto a fire.

"I told you it won't work. All you're doing is feeding the witches of Crystal Point Island your power."

"The witches of Crystal Point Island? What are you talking about? There aren't any witches on this island," she said, wondering if she'd been sucked into a parallel universe.

"There are, Sage. They're angry, and they'll stop at nothing to regain control of this rock," he said, sounding exhausted.

"Why did they lose it? Did you take that, too?" she shot back as anger filled every inch of her being. It was starting to sink in that she'd been abducted and taken to the most cliché dungeon one could imagine. Seriously? It looked like something right out of a villain's playbook.

"No, but my wife did. By accident," he said and glanced away, looking pained.

"Your wife? The one in Salem?" Wasn't that what August had told her? That he'd followed his second wife across the country when he was just a teenager?

"No, not Sissy. Carrie, August's mom. It's the reason all of this is happening now." The man's expression was haggard and resigned. He had the look of someone who had accepted his fate. Whatever that might be.

She sat back against the wall and took a deep breath, trying to process what was happening. Somehow, she'd gotten caught up in some war between the West family and some witches she'd never heard of. Why? She had no idea. All she knew was that she'd slept with a man for the first time in over three years, and the next morning she'd ended up in a dungeon with his father.

Wasn't that just perfect? Now she remembered why she preferred to stay in her studio instead of "enjoying life" as her grandmother had put it. If this was what she got after one night of fun, then she'd gladly swear off men forever.

August's face flashed in her mind, his smile easy and his eyes filled with mischief. There was no denying that everything about him had filled her with joy. Spending time with him had become her happy place, and she never wanted to give that up. Her eyes welled with tears, and her heart ached with the idea that she might never see him again.

But he betrayed you, another voice chimed in.

She shook her head, unable to make sense of the conflicting emotions threatening to tear her up from the inside out.

"Sage, listen—" Phillip started, but footsteps sounded on the stone floor, and he went silent.

"What horror do I have to look forward to next?" Sage muttered as she peered down the dark passage.

"I'm glad you asked, Ms. Easton," a woman said as she emerged from the darkness. It was the same woman with the icy voice that she'd met in the woods that morning.

"Well? I'm waiting," Sage said defiantly.

"Your attitude won't serve you here, Sage Easton. Nobody here cares who your family is."

The hell they didn't. Otherwise the woman wouldn't keep using her surname. "No? Then why was I taken? What is it you hope to get from me?"

"Not from you," she said, staring Sage down as if she were trying to read Sage's reactions. "From your boyfriend. Once he returns what is ours, you'll be free to go... assuming you cooperate of course."

"Boyfriend?" she asked. "I don't have a boyfriend. You have the wrong girl." Sage tugged on her restraints, fruitlessly trying to get free.

The woman in the cloak snorted, showing the first trace of

emotion. "We'll see." She turned her attention to Phillip. "It won't be long now. If we know anything about your boy, it's that he's loyal. Well, loyal to those who are loyal to him."

Phillip let out a growl and threw himself forward as if he were going to attack her, but of course the chains yanked him back, rendering him harmless.

The woman in the cloak let out a haunting laugh. Immediately vines started growing out of the stone walls, covering the space so thoroughly that it looked more like an enchanted garden instead of the stone dungeon. Even Sage's restraints turned to purple silk ropes that matched the large blooms that had appeared on the vines.

Sage stared at the spectacle, wondering why the witch was wasting her magic on the illusion. As soon as she realized it was, in fact, an illusion, all of the stage dressing vanished, and Sage realized they were in a regular house that had stains on the walls and ceiling. It looked like it had suffered a leak at some point but was never fixed. The floors were old brown carpet, and across the room was a kitchen that looked straight out of the sixties with its olive-green appliances and yellow cabinets.

She tugged again at the restraints, hopeful that they might pull right out of the sheetrock, but no such luck. Whoever had bolted them in definitely knew how to find the studs.

"You won't be free until your boyfriend and his father returns what is ours," the woman said. "It'd be easier for you if you didn't resist."

"You think I'm not going to resist being chained to the wall? You've lost your mind, lady," Sage said, her voice full of rage.

The woman ignored her and started to walk back into the darkness.

"What exactly do you think August has of yours?" Sage called after her.

The woman paused and glanced back at Sage. She'd morphed from a beautiful young woman to one who had aged significantly with crow's feet around her eyes and papery thin skin. "He has the key to our magic. We intend to get it back."

She turned back around and disappeared into the darkness once more. Only this time, it wasn't down a stone tunnel. It was down the hall of the shabby home that looked like it hadn't been lived in for decades.

Honestly, Sage preferred the stone and fire illusion and welcomed it back into her consciousness. It was less depressing. If she never saw the shoddy house again, it would be too soon.

Sage turned her attention to Phillip. "Do you know what she was talking about? That August has the key to their magic? What key?"

He nodded once and then closed his eyes, looking pained.

"Phillip! What happens when he gives them the key?"

"He can't give it to them. They have to take it," Phillip said, his voice dull. "And when they do, he will die."

CHAPTER 24

"Sage!" August cried as he ran after her. "Please, wait!"

But she didn't turn around. She only ran faster. Everything inside of him screamed for him to chase her down, to explain the unexplainable. To try to reason with her and make her understand why he was still in contact with the woman she thought had been the cause of her mother's death.

Everyone in Keating Hollow had blamed Ophelia for Dahlia Easton's death. Even after Ophelia's name had been cleared, she'd never been able to shake those allegations. It was likely she never would. It was why she'd moved to Port Townsend not long after the tragic incident.

August hadn't always known where she was, but after his mother's death, he'd found a letter asking him to go visit her once a week. His mother felt someone needed to keep an eye on her since her magic was diminished, and she'd be a target should anyone find her. She'd said Ophelia had once saved her life, and no matter what the town thought, Ophelia was a good witch and deserved the benefit of the doubt.

He hadn't questioned his mother's last wishes. He'd just

gone to see her, and after a few visits, he'd started to enjoy his time with her. Her days of magic wielding were pretty much behind her, and as far as August could tell, the only magic she used these days was to heat the tea in her mug after it cooled.

But Sage wouldn't want to hear any of that. Not now. Maybe not ever. He grimaced, praying to the gods that he was wrong and that she'd come around once she had time to process.

"August, we don't have time for this," Ophelia said from behind him. "Your father is in danger."

He spun around to face the older woman, and it was then that he realized she was dressed in stylish jeans and a high-waisted top that really flattered her figure. It was a far cry from the track suits he was used to seeing her in when he went to visit. "Ophelia, what exactly is going on here?"

"I told you, it's your father. He—"

"Yeah, I heard you the first time. He's in danger. So? He was probably stealing magic again." He waved at her. "I meant all this. You're wearing clothes that don't make you look eighty. And for some reason, you keep in contact with my dad. Why?"

"A lady can change her look anytime she wants to, August. I hardly think my wardrobe choices are important at the moment. Right now, we need to get started on casting a spell to protect your dad, and then we need to get you out of here."

He frowned at her. "What do you mean? Since when do I cast spells?"

"Since now." She grabbed his hand and started to haul him back to the house.

But August resisted and pulled his hand from hers, looking at her as if he'd never seen her before. "I'm not concerned with helping my father. Whatever he's gotten into, he can get himself out of it. I don't mess around with magic. You know that. I'm not going to start now." He turned, determined to go find Sage. He knew she was upset, but he wasn't going to let her walk all the way home. And especially not when it was through the woods in the early dawn light.

He took off, calling her name. And when he finally spotted her, she was standing near the tree line, her face white. He called her name again and took off in her direction, but before he could even take his second step, someone in a cloak appeared behind her. Suddenly Sage's body went limp in the person's arms.

"Sage!" he cried again and ran toward her, but he was too far away. The person in the cloak stuffed Sage's body onto a four-wheeler and took off through the woods.

He ran as far and as fast as he could, trying to see where the four-wheeler had gone, but when he got to the tree line, there weren't any tracks, nor could he hear the roar of the engine. It was as if the four-wheeler, Sage, and her abductor had all vanished into thin air.

August let out a roar of frustration and tried to ignore the feeling of helplessness that nearly paralyzed him.

What had just happened? Ophelia had shown up, looking very much like someone completely different than the older woman he visited every week. His father was apparently in danger, and now Sage had been abducted.

There was only one thing to do.

He went back to his house, where he ignored Ophelia's pleas for his cooperation, jumped into his truck, and jammed the key into the ignition. Before he could peel out of the driveway, Ophelia hopped into the passenger seat and said, "You can't do this, August. You just can't."

He cast her an irritated glance as he slammed the truck into Drive and hightailed it out to the highway.

"You don't understand the consequences. If you tell the coven, they'll only offer you up as bait to get Sage back."

He frowned at her. "What do some rogue witches want with me?"

She bit down on her bottom lip and appeared to be debating with herself about what to tell him.

"You know what? It doesn't matter. I'm more than willing to sacrifice myself in order to keep Sage safe. So either get on board or get out. Your choice."

"August!" she cried. "You can't. Don't you understand? Once they start siphoning their magic, you will die, and then Sage's mother will have died for nothing."

He slammed on the breaks, stopping just shy of Witch Tower Road. "What?"

She sighed and leaned back in the seat, looking as if she hadn't slept in a week. "There's something you need to know."

"I'm waiting." He had zero patience for waiting to hear whatever she'd been hiding from him.

"It started when your mom was a teenager. She and Dahlia Easton, Befana at the time, were on Crystal Point Island. Back in those days, the place was rich with magic, the kind that seeps from cave walls and bubbles up from natural springs. It was said that Crystal Point Island magic was pure and would boost a witch's abilities. The short version is that Dahlia dared Carrie to cast a spell so that she'd be just as powerful as the Befana family."

"I take it the spell didn't go as planned?" August asked.

"Yes. And no. The spell worked. Your mother became a very powerful witch. Not at first, but over the years, she kept siphoning the magic from the island until the magic became very unstable. She wasn't trying to; it was the spell she cast. And when she tried to undo it, it was too late. The magic of the island was too unstable. There was nowhere to store it, so it stayed with Carrie. Until you were born."

Unease washed over him, and he was fairly sure he didn't want to hear what she said next. "I'm guessing by your tone that isn't good news."

She shook her head. "It isn't. Once you were born, the spell transferred to you, and you've been siphoning their magic ever since."

He shook his head, certain that she was having some sort of mental episode. "That's not possible. My only ability is talking to animals and a little minor talent with water magic."

"It's not, August. The only reason you think that is because I've been neutralizing your magic for years now. Ever since Dahlia's tragic accident."

"She didn't die from a love spell gone wrong, did she?" he asked, looking at her in a whole different light.

"No, August. She died trying to shield you from siphoning magic. The thing is it worked. Her spell is still good today. You no longer siphon magic, but you do shed it. And that's what I do once a week. I neutralize it."

He wasn't quite sure what to make of everything she was saying. How could he know if it was the truth? Other than his mother's letters claiming that Ophelia was like family and that he could trust her. How had he thought she was just a harmless older witch who spent her days cultivating her garden and having dinner with him once a week? This woman was much more animated and vibrant than the one he knew from his visits. Had it all been some sort of act?

He cocked his head to the side and eyed her with suspicion. "If all of that is true, then why does everyone think it's your fault Dahlia died? They still think it was a love spell gone bad."

"Because Dahlia told her mother that she was casting me a

love spell that night when she went to try to free you from that spell. She thought it was her fault since she was the one who dared your mom to do that spell all those years ago. Once they realized you were involved, Dahlia was determined to break it. But it was too much for her, and the spell drained her life force. After that, the official story was love spell gone bad, and everyone blamed me. I could've tried to set the record straight, but if I'd done that, everyone would've found out about your ability, and that would have put you in danger. I took the fall to protect you both. I loved your mother like a sister. I'd have done anything for her."

"It sounds like you have," he said, rubbing the ache in his forehead. "Where does my dad fit into all of this?"

"Oh honey, he's not perfect, but that business with the magic... He was trying to load up to help you. That's why he siphoned magic from the bay. You've been shedding more magic than usual lately. I told him, and he came back, determined to be ready for when the island witches came for you."

"Why would they come for me?" he asked, gripping the truck's steering wheel so hard his knuckles were white.

"Because, August, they can feel you shedding their magic. And now that they know you are carrying it around with you, they want it back. That's why they took Sage. The only way for them to take it back from you is for you to offer it. They want a trade."

The choice was simple. He didn't want their magic. He only wanted Sage. "Fine. They can have it. And then they can let Sage go."

"August!" she said sharply. "Haven't you been paying attention? If they take the magic back, it will kill you. You can't trade the magic for Sage. It's your *life*. I can't let that happen. I promised your mother. If you do this, Dahlia will have given her life for nothing."

"If I don't do this, Dahlia's daughter will die because of me," he said, his voice calm but full of conviction. "I won't let that happen. You can either come with me or get out now. Your choice."

"August—"

"I'm sorry, Ophelia. But Sage has a family who loves her. She has a successful business to run. What do I have? A house? A few part time jobs? If it's a choice between me and her, there's no question."

"You don't understand, August."

"I do understand. She'll live and I won't. Is there anything else?"

"Dammit." There were tears in her eyes as she slowly opened the door and slid out. "I won't go and watch you kill yourself, August. I won't."

He gave her a nod, his entire body numb with shock. But then just before she closed the door, he said, "Thank you for telling me all this. And thank you for everything else. Here I thought I was taking care of you, but instead, it was the other way around, wasn't it?"

She nodded, tears streaming down her face. "I'm sorry I failed."

"You didn't. It's not your fault. You did what you had to do, and now I have to do the same. Take care, Ophelia."

"Take care, August. I love you." As soon as the words were out of her mouth, she clicked the door closed and walked toward town, her head down with disappointment radiating from her.

He hesitated for only a second before speeding off down the street toward Devil's Cauldron Bridge.

CHAPTER 25

SAGE STARED open-mouthed at Phillip West, wondering if anything he'd just told her was true. Her mom had died trying to save August? It hadn't been a love spell but a siphoning spell that had been suggested by her own mother that she'd tried to rectify years later?

"You're saying that we're both here because we're bait?" she asked him.

Phillip snorted. "Yes. Though they underestimated how much disdain my son has for me. So they had to find someone else he cares about to lure him here."

"And then what? He lets them have their magic back and they let us all go?" That didn't seem likely considering the witches had already abducted two people.

"In theory, they let us go. August..." He swallowed thickly. "He'd give his life for ours."

"No!" she said automatically, her insides churning with so much turmoil, she thought she might vomit. "They'll kill him?"

"They won't. The spell will. You see, Sage, he was born with the power to siphon the magic from this island. If they take it from him, a core piece of who he is will be taken. He won't survive it."

"He can't come here," she said with conviction. "We'll just have to find a way out."

Phillip looked about eighty years old when he let out a long sigh and turned to stare into the darkness. "There's no way out," he said, sounding defeated. "I've tried."

"Not nearly enough," she muttered and tried once again to send magic to the restraints cuffing her to the wall. Once again, it just seeped into the steel, frustrating her.

Her mind started to wander to that morning when Ophelia had shown up. At the time, she'd been convinced that August had betrayed her. But after hearing Phillip's explanation, she now knew that everything she'd been told about her mother's death was a lie. And when she'd run, she'd run right into the Crystal Point Island witches, and she'd sealed her own fate. Would anything have been different if she'd stayed and let him explain? Maybe, maybe not. Phillip said that even August didn't know the truth. They'd still have been blind to the real problem.

Both of their mothers had made questionable choices, and now they'd have to pay the price. But not the ultimate one. Not if Sage had anything to say about it. One way or another, if August showed up to save her from this hellhole, she wouldn't be leaving without him. She'd never forgive herself if she did.

She just needed to find a way to wield her magic without it being siphoned off.

Siphoned. Normally, magic didn't just bleed from people. August might be a special case, but she wasn't. If her magic was being taken, there was something that was taking it. She just had to figure out what.

The shackles? That was a strong possibility. Every time she

tried to free herself, the magic seemed to be swallowed up by them. Until she was free, she couldn't know for sure. Was there another possibility? She studied the stone cave and tried to force herself to see it as it truly was. A regular house that hadn't been maintained or updated in a number of years.

Sitting against the wall, she pressed her hand to the damp sheetrock and let her eyes go unfocused. Sure enough, the illusion started to fade, and she was able to make out the room. It was empty except for Phillip and herself. She scowled and nearly let the illusion creep back in, but then she saw it.

It was faint enough that anyone who didn't know what they were looking at would likely miss it. But not Sage. Not the granddaughter of the Befana Bay coven leader.

Right there in the middle of the room was the outline of a pentagram. It was small, but she could see just a faint trace of magic lighting up the edges.

That was it. That was where the magic was being siphoned from her.

If she could get to it, rough up the chalk outline, then she'd have a fighting chance. She just had to get out of the damned shackles.

She stared down at her hands, noted the red chaff marks, and had to tamp down the anger that roared up, nearly choking her. Unable to contain herself, she yanked at the cuffs again, this time hard enough to break the skin on her wrist. Blood seeped out from under the cuff, causing a spark of magic the moment the blood hit the steel.

Sage studied the cuffs, wondering what just happened. Her blood had created a visible spark of magic instead of just fading out like it did when she called it up from inside of her. Blood magic was frowned upon in the community. It was powerful and not easily controlled. But if there was ever a time to throw the rules out the window, it was in that moment.

She moved her wrist against the cuff, causing more sparks to erupt, only to just watch them peter out.

Frustrated, she wiggled her wrist and then pressed it against the floor, forcing the cuff into her flesh hard enough that she winced. A trickle of blood appeared beneath the cuff. This time instead of just letting her blood touch the stainless steel, she envisioned the blood encircling her wrist, acting as protection from all things evil.

Very slowly her blood inched its way around her wrist. She kept her eyes trained on her blood, willing it to connect in a full circle. To create a space that would serve as protection from having her magic siphoned. "Come on," she whispered, coaxing it to bend to her will.

Magic sparked from her cuff, shocking her and making her wince with pain. Her concentration was broken and so was the connection to her blood that she needed to get it to do what she asked of it.

"Son of..." She gritted her teeth and tried again, unwilling to give up. This time, the blood connected almost instantly, and Sage wondered what had made the difference. It didn't matter. She had what she needed.

"Are you ready, Phillip?" she asked Austin's dad.

"Ready for what?" he asked without even looking at her.

"To get out of this place."

He turned, met her eyes, and frowned. "There's no getting out. Not unless August—"

Sage raised her arm, showed him the blood circle around her wrist, and then slammed her wrist down on the floor as she cried, "Set me free!"

There was a loud crackle, followed by the stench of burned flesh.

"Holy hell, Sage. What did you do?" he asked.

She glanced down, taking in the dark burn marks circling her wrists, and then smiled when she realized it had worked. The cuffs were gone. She held her arms out and said, "Your turn."

His eyes were wide with shock, and he seemed to not be able to form words.

Sage didn't wait for his approval. Instead, she moved to his side, grabbed one of his wrists, and stabbed a fingernail into his skin, making him bleed. When she tried to force the blood to coat his entire wrist, there was resistance she wasn't expecting.

What was holding her back now?

The pentagram. Of course.

She ran over to the area where she'd noted the pentagram and softened her gaze, waiting for the illusion to fade. It finally appeared in a faint outline. She quickly used her foot to smear the drawing, knowing it would weaken the symbol.

Once she was sure she'd caused enough damage, she ran back over to Phillip and ordered his blood to encircle his wrist. It did so instantly.

Sage let out a huge sigh of relief. Her magic was back. She touched the steel cuffs he still wore and envisioned them broken on the ground. A second later, the cuffs fell off, and Phillip was free.

He held his hands up, awe etched in his tired features. "You did it. How?"

"Later," she said. "Right now, we need to get the eff out of here."

She helped him to his feet, and the pair of them headed

toward the dark hallway. But before they could make their escape, the auburn-haired woman appeared, and this time she wasn't alone. Right behind her there were two large bodyguard types restraining August.

They were too late. He'd already come to exchange himself for them.

Sage's heart nearly broke in two as she saw the expression on August's face. It was one of regret but filled with resolve. He was ready to lay down his life to save hers.

"I see you managed to shed your restraints," the witch said, sounding unconcerned. "It doesn't matter now. Once I start siphoning our magic back, you won't be able to stop it."

"We'll see about that," Sage shot back without any clue as to how she'd be able to help once an altercation went down. All she knew was that no one was taking August from her. One way or another, she'd make sure of that.

"Let them go," August said. "You have me. That was the deal."

"I don't think so," the witch said. "Not until we're sure you can give us what we need."

"That wasn't the deal, Barbie," August hissed.

"It doesn't matter," Sage said, holding August's gaze. "Because I'm not leaving here without you."

"Sage, no. Don't make this harder than it has to be. I just want you safe," he said.

"I will be," she promised. Then she turned to... "Barbie, is it?"

The witch rolled her eyes but said nothing.

Sage took it as confirmation. "Listen, Barbie. We can do this the easy way or the hard way. You can either let August go so he can leave with us, or you can invite a full-on witch battle. Think carefully, because I'm an Easton, and we were blessed with more power than you ever dreamed of."

"You think so?" she asked calmly.

"I know so." There was so much hubris in Sage's statements, but they were playing for keeps. If she could intimidate the other witch, it was worth a shot.

"I'd like to see you try, Easton," Barbie said and then turned and grasped onto August, her fingers digging into his flesh as if she were going to fillet him alive.

"What the hell, you crazy bitch!" Sage launched herself at the other witch, grabbed hold of her arms and yanked. Only the witch wasn't budging, and neither was August.

Barbie stood perfectly still, her claws locked on August as magic flowed freely from him and into her. When Sage paid close attention, she could almost see the magic pooling just under the witch's skin.

Something snapped in Sage's mind, and it was as if she were back in her studio, manipulating magic with her glass work. Her mind focused on that magic, the ball of it building up under Barbie's skin, and the next thing Sage knew, she was forcing it out of the witch.

The ball of magic hovered just between the two of them, each of them connected, but neither able to do anything with the magic. They were just trapped there until one of them broke free or Sage broke the connection.

Sage stood perilously close to Barbie. "What will you do if I just destroy this magic?"

"You can't," the witch said through clenched teeth. "It will be the end of my people."

"So ending your people is off limits, but killing one of mine isn't?"

"He has our magic!" she snarled.

"Maybe. But he didn't take it on purpose. It's not his fault. Yet you want to end the life of the most helpful, kind, gracious person I've ever met. For what? So you are able to cast spells again? Is it really worth a person's life?"

"You wouldn't want to live without your magic," Barbie countered.

"True. I wouldn't. But I certainly wouldn't kill anyone just so that I could have the power to sell glass lamps that never burn out." Sage nodded to Phillip. "Find me a container with a lid. Preferably a glass jar."

He just stared at her.

"Phillip, now!" she cried, wondering how August had put up with him for so long.

The older man turned and hurried into the old kitchen. It wasn't long before he handed Sage a large glass jar and produced a lid marked *Danger*.

"No kidding," Sage muttered before staring Barbie in the eye and saying, "Last chance. Cooperate now and you'll get out of this unscathed. Put up a fight and there's no telling what will happen to you."

The other witch growled at Sage and then turned almost feral as she tried to reclaim the magic still suspended between them. She was grabbing at it, screaming that the magic was hers, and snarling in everyone's direction. The two men who were holding August hostage actually took a few steps back, though they didn't release him.

From a distance, she heard shouts and cries that sounded a lot like a battle was going on outside. Magic was crackling in the air, and it wasn't the magic that had come from August.

Sage didn't know how much time she had before other witches found them. She had her power back, and although it was formidable, she couldn't ward off multiple attackers at once. It was now or never.

She handed the lid to Phillip and said, "Be ready."

He just nodded, staring at her with awe.

Sage focused on the ball of magic still tethered to both August and Barbie. The magic was old with thick bonds that didn't seem to want to leave either of them. The magic had found a home in August, but it still remembered the witches of Crystal Point Island and wanted to be with them, too. "Maybe later," she said to no one, and then she set her magic free.

The bright white light of Sage's magic flew to the ball suspended between the two witches, and it immediately started pulsing. The beat was Sage's magic, and she sighed in relief when she realized this was going to work. All she had to do was coax the magic into the jar.

Only when she commanded the ball to move, it didn't. Instead, it reached for Barbie, and if Sage didn't stop it, she'd get Sage's magic too.

She would not let that happen!

Sage charged them, her magic flowing freely from her straight into the magical ball. She filled it with so much magic that it was impossible for Barbie to keep up. That was fine. Her main goal was to keep Barbie occupied while she freed August from the terrible bond his mother had created for him all those years ago.

Using her mind's eye, she let her magic probe his, searching for a way that August's magic could be separated from the magic of the island witches.

August groaned and was starting to sink to his knees when she finally felt it. There was a line between his magic and the coven's. Sage was quick to sever the link. The magic ball Barbie had fought for so hard was now toast, and the remnants of that magic fell into the glass jar at her feet. With a flick of her wrist, the lid flew out of Phillip's hands and attached itself to the jar, trapping the rogue magic.

Barbie was on her knees, weeping that she'd failed again, while August climbed to his feet and headed straight toward Sage.

"I knew you were special," he said as he hugged her tightly.

"I knew you were, too. I just didn't know how special," she said with a tiny laugh. "Want to get out of here?"

"Gladly." They held on tightly to each other as they made their way out of the shabby house. All around them, they could feel the carnage of spells and echoes of betrayals. The island witches had fought, and if Sage wasn't so drained from her own magic manipulation, she would have instantly noticed that her grandmother, all three of her sisters, and August's grandmother Serena were all there.

They all turned in a line, looking disheveled but happy when they spotted Sage and August walking out of the old house under their own power with Phillip trailing them.

Tears sprang to Sage's eyes. Her family had shown up, no questions asked.

"Sage?" her grandmother said, sounding worried. "Are you all right? We came as soon as Ophelia told us you were taken."

"I am now." She threw her arms around the woman who'd helped raised her and was grateful for her love and support.

"And August?" Bethany Befana asked. "He'll need a medical examination."

"We'll get one, but for now he's alive, and that's what counts."

Her sisters surrounded her, each of them touching her with love. Her heart was full as she looked at her family and friends.

"Yeah. I'm here, and that's what counts," August said from

behind her. "Now, can we go? I seem to recall we were interrupted this morning before we could finish... that game we were working on."

"Yes," she said instantly, wanting to be curled in his arms more than anything after the morning they'd had.

August turned to his own grandmother and asked, "Is tomorrow okay for that catch-up we need?"

Serena reached out and squeezed his arm. "Tomorrow is perfect." Then she kissed his cheek and was gone before anyone could even clock that she'd left.

The Eastons, however, were a different story. Her three sisters were insisting that Sage go home with one of them. When she kept refusing, there was a small mutiny because they thought she needed to be in a house with witches who could protect her.

She declined each one of them and then let August take her to his home in the woods, where she decided that if she never left, it would be too soon.

CHAPTER 26

"Have you thought anymore about Silas's offer?" Sage asked August as they strolled along the shoreline hand in hand in the late afternoon. It had been roughly two weeks since the battle with the witches of Crystal Point Island. Since that day, they'd mostly laid low at August's house, trying to process everything that had gone down. They'd done a lot of talking and then spent a lot of time in comfortable silence. It was one of August's favorite things about dating Sage. They could both talk about everything and anything, but they were just as comfortable in the silence.

"I have," he said hesitantly.

She paused and looked up at him. "You're nervous. Why?"

He ran a hand through his hair and stared out at the water, not sure how to articulate his feelings. "I'm not nervous so much as just frustrated with myself. I know I need to give Silas an answer, but I don't know what to say."

"Tell me your thoughts." She started walking again, and he was grateful. He always thought better when he was moving.

"It's a great opportunity, and if it was here in Befana Bay, I'd have already said yes."

"But you're hesitant because it's in Keating Hollow, right?" she asked.

"Yes." He looked out over the bay, taking in the soft pinks and oranges that had appeared as the sun started to set. "I've never spent much time away from Befana Bay before. I always told myself it was because of Ophelia, but the truth is that every time I left, I felt an emptiness that had me wishing I'd never taken the out-of-town job. All I wanted to do was get back home."

"Because you missed someone here or you just felt unsettled?" she asked.

"Unsettled. I missed my grandmother Serena and was anxious about Ophelia, but only because I was trying to fulfill a duty to my mom. It's not like I missed her."

"Hmm, interesting. Maybe it was the magic that was tied to you. That would do it. It wanted to be here, near Crystal Point Island, and the further away you got, the more unsettled you were."

"Maybe," he said with a nod, knowing deep in his gut that she was right. He'd always gotten that emptiness as soon as he left town. He'd never understood it before. But now that Sage had cleansed him of the island's magic, his anxiety about travel had all but disappeared. "There's another reason I don't want to be gone for five or six months."

Sage smiled up at him. "Let me guess, you don't want to be away from Kelly that long."

August let out a bark of laughter. It had become a running joke with them that August was pining for his roommate. Kelly had gotten back to town a week ago, and the first thing he'd said when he walked in the door was that August could stop moping now because he was home. That, combined with Sage's misunderstanding that August was into his roommate, had been an endless source of fodder for them.

"You got me. I don't want to leave Kelly. He might make a move on my girl."

"You go on one trip to the outlets with a guy, and the next thing you know, your boyfriend is worried they'll run off together," she teased. Then she sobered. "What's the real reason you don't want to leave?"

He shook his head and cast her a sidelong glance. "Come on, Sage. You know why."

"Because of me?"

"Of course. We just started this. Is it so terrible that I don't want to be gone for five or six months?" he asked, now fully facing her, waiting for her answer.

She reached up and placed her hands on his chest. "So if it weren't for me, you'd go?"

He didn't like where this was going. "Maybe."

"Maybe? I thought we were going to be honest with each other," she said with an air of disappointment.

"Fine." He tucked her hair behind her ear, loving that he was allowed to do that. "Yes, I'd do it. It's my dream job working with one of my favorite people. Why wouldn't I?"

She grinned up at him. "Was that so hard?"

"Yes." He gave her a soft smile.

"What if I told you I was considering taking some time off during the winter? That if you went to Keating Hollow for months, and if I were invited, I'd like to go with you?"

He blinked down at her. "You? Leave for months? What about your store?"

"I know. It sounds crazy. But I actually did learn something while I was away from my shop. I don't have to be there twenty-four seven and the store still runs. Who knew? My assistant does a fine job of keeping the lights on without me." She dropped her hand and stared at the rocky beach for a moment. "The truth is that I've never spent time anywhere but Befana Bay. I think maybe it's time to see a little bit of the outside world. I'd like to do that with you. I'll just make extra inventory so there's product for the shelves. If I have to come back to work for a bit, I can do that and then turn around again to go be with you."

"You're serious about this, aren't you?" he asked, his heart filling with love for the beautiful creature in front of him.

"I am." She stepped forward and wrapped her arms around him. "You're the best thing that's ever happened to me. You're there for me in ways no one else has ever been. I want to be the same for you."

"You might just be the best thing that's happened to me, too," he said, wondering what had taken him so long when it came to Sage Easton. She'd been right there in front of him for years, but until a few weeks ago, he'd been blind to how perfect she was for him. "I have a hard time imagining you not working for months. What would you even do? You may have learned some things about work-life balance, but I can't imagine you being idle for months. You'd go crazy."

Sage got a sheepish smile and then threw her hands up as she said, "Okay, you're right. I can't not work. I was thinking of maybe opening a second gallery and studio in Keating Hollow. I could hire an assistant, someone who is looking to showcase their work, and we'd share store space. I'd be able to blow glass while we're there and you'd get to further your career. It's a win-win, right?"

He was silent for a long moment before he pulled her into his arms again and held her against him. "You're incredible."

"I know," she said with a laugh. "Now if only I could talk you into letting me sell some of that artwork in the garage…"

He chuckled, his chest rumbling. "We'll talk about that later."

She pulled back quickly and stared up at him, surprise all over her perfect face. "Don't tease me, August. Are you seriously thinking about that?"

He nodded. "You're right. If people want them, then they should be out in the world. Plus, a wise person told me that if I let them go, I'll make room in my life for new work. I think she might have been onto something."

"Oh my gosh! I'm so excited." She started rattling off all the things she planned to do to sell his artwork.

August half listened, content to just see how animated she was. Creating and selling artwork truly was her passion. Working was always going to give her a rush, and it filled his heart to see her so excited. If she was always like that when it came to his work, he'd probably start making things just to see that light shining in her eyes. For him, art was all about experiencing a moment in time. Handing something over to her and having her radiate with joy at the idea of sharing it with the world was a moment he'd love to relive over and over and over again.

"I've lost you, haven't I?" Sage asked with amusement.

"A little," he admitted. "I was too busy being entertained by your excitement to listen to the details. I'm sure whatever you said was brilliant."

"So posing naked for the local artists a couple times a month would be okay with you then? That would be one hell of a draw. We'll hold the classes in the gallery so that—"

"Wait, what? You think I'm going to pose nude just to get people to pay attention to my art? Sage, I don't—"

She burst out laughing. "That's one way to get you to listen to me." She winked at him. "You won't be posing for anyone but me from here on out. I don't share. Understood?"

"Understood," he said and leaned down, kissing her so thoroughly that they were both breathing hard when they finally pulled away.

"Wow. Uh, what were we talking about?" Sage asked him.

"Art. But right now we need to get to your grandmother's house for that dinner."

"Right." She grabbed his hand and said, "Better hurry or we'll be on dishes duty."

August shrugged. "I don't mind."

"I do. You haven't seen that woman cook. The last time I had to clean, she had food on the ceiling. Do you know how hard it is to get food off a fifteen-foot ceiling?"

"We'll manage," he said, far too content to worry about a thing.

CHAPTER 27

AUGUST WAS SO relaxed and content with his recent decisions that he didn't even notice the person waiting on Bethany's porch until they were almost to the door.

"Hello, son," Phillip said, startling him.

Instinctively, August squeezed Sage's hand as he turned to his father. "What are you doing here?"

"I wanted to talk to you before I head Back East."

He released Sage's hand and crossed his arms over his chest. "Fine. Talk."

Sage cleared her throat and said, "Maybe I should give you two some privacy."

August nodded once, indicating that he'd heard her. He briefly considered asking her to stay, but if he lost it on his father, he didn't want to subject her to his anger. Not after the afternoon they'd spent together.

Once Sage was inside, Phillip gestured for August to sit across from him in one of the porch chairs.

August shook his head. "This conversation won't last that long."

Phillip let out a long sigh. "I suppose I deserve that. I just wanted to apologize to you for the way that everything went down. I know I didn't handle things well. After your mother died, I didn't know how to parent you. So I didn't. I just bailed. There's no excuse for that. But later, when we learned that your powers were shedding, I tried to come back and rectify that. To keep the island witches from finding out. I only ever siphoned magic so that I could mask what was going on with you when Ophelia was struggling to neutralize your magic. I didn't mean to mess with the town's magic source. I understand now that Sage's power didn't come back because of me."

"Her magic is fine now," August said. "Bethany said that with all the heightened emotions over on Crystal Point Island, her magic broke through all the barriers then and it's been fine ever since."

"That's good. I'm really glad to hear that. Bethany told me that by siphoning the magic from the bay I upset the balance of the town, and that's why everything was going haywire. Especially when Sage was around, because her powers were trying to find their way back to her. It's why your uncle Bruce thought she was responsible for the magic there going wonky. He could feel her power struggling to right itself."

August had forgotten all about Bruce and his special brand of crazy. "You saw Bruce?"

He nodded. "I went out there to see how he's doing. His land is flush with power these days. The old family kind that builds up when witches live there for a number of years. It would be a good place for spellcasting."

August narrowed his eyes at him. "Is that what you were doing? Spellcasting?"

He shook his head. "I'm done with that. I only ever wanted to protect you, son. I hope you can believe me."

August didn't. Not really. He'd always believe his father was looking for an easy way to spell himself into a better situation. But he did believe that his father had wanted to protect him. Why else would he have come back right when August needed him most, and why was he still in Befana Bay if he wasn't trying to make amends? In fact, if he was trying to do anything shady, he wouldn't be at Bethany Befana's house at all. He wasn't sure what to say, so he settled on, "I hope you mean that."

"I do. And I just hope we can work on rebuilding a relationship. When you're ready of course."

August took a deep breath and closed his eyes, knowing that if he refused his father this request, it was likely they'd never reconcile. After everything that had happened, he wasn't ready to cut that cord. "Sure, Dad. You just need to give me some time."

Phillip blew out a long breath and nodded, looking relieved. "Of course. When you're ready." He stood and held his arms out. "Can I get a hug for your old dad?"

"Yeah, okay." August let his dad wrap his arms around him and hesitated for just a second before hugging him back. It was weird and awkward, but also cathartic in a way. He didn't know what the future held for them, but he did know he was at least willing to try. "Love you, Dad."

His father sounded choked up when he said, "Love you, too, son."

Phillip's eyes were misty when he let August go. "I better take off and let you get on with your dinner."

It was weird sending his father off when Sage's entire

family was inside, gathered together for a family dinner. "Did you want to stay?"

"No, no," he said, waving his hands. "I don't want to intrude." Then he slipped off the porch and started to head into town. As August watched him, he couldn't help noticing when his father wiped at his eyes. His heart ached a little at the thought of his father in pain. He knew there was nothing he could do about it now, but maybe, just maybe, there was hope for the two of them after all.

August quietly slipped into the house and came up short when he saw Ophelia and Sage talking. They were holding hands and having an intense conversation.

His grandmother Serena stepped up beside him and said, "I really wasn't sure she was going to come. Bethany invited her, but after all these years, I wouldn't have blamed her for writing this entire town off."

"She'd never do that," August said. "She loves it too much. What are they talking about?"

"Sage is apologizing for the way everyone treated her. And Ophelia is apologizing for not trusting anyone with the truth," Serena said. "Though it's not all on her. I knew, too, and I never said anything."

August stared down at his grandmother, shocked. "You did?"

"Of course I did. It took a village to keep you safe." She grabbed his hand and held it with both of hers. "You know Ophelia called me the moment your father showed up and siphoned that magic. I was all the way in Australia, halfway around the world. But I'm glad she called, because otherwise I wouldn't have been here to help Bethany and the coven get you out of that ridiculous, mold-infested house turned dungeon."

"I'm glad you were here, Gran. I don't think I'd have survived the last few weeks without you."

"You would have. But it's good to have family around when things are rough. It's why you really should reconcile with your dad," she said without judgment.

"You really think so? I have you and Ophelia."

"And Sage," she added for good measure. "But you can never have too many people who care about you. Think on it."

"I will." But it wasn't the only thing he'd been thinking about lately. "Do you know what's happening with the witches of Crystal Point Island?" It was something none of them had talked about much since that night. Neither August nor Sage had wanted to relive it, but if he was going to move forward with his life, he needed to know what to expect from them. He'd been their target for so long, he just couldn't convince himself that they'd finally leave him alone.

"I do know," she said, turning to him. "I was just waiting for you to ask about it."

"I'm ready."

"The leaders of that coven have all been arrested. The magic that your mother tapped into was illegal and should never have been there for the taking. The fact that they were dabbling in forbidden magic and then abducted both Phillip and Sage means they won't be free for a long, long time. I learned that the Magical Task Force has been investigating them since Dahlia's death, but they hadn't gotten anything concrete until now. That community is fractured, and in the coming years, it will need to be rebuilt with younger witches who were never a part of the old coven. The Befana Bay coven has committed to taking them under their wing. With any luck, they'll be a thriving witch community just like ours within a few short years."

"That's… remarkable," August said. "Do you think they'll be able to move past that history and become something better?"

"Sure, August. Do you really think Befana Bay never had their share of nefarious witches? There are dishonorable people in every community. It doesn't mean the others can't rise above." She patted his hand and said, "We'll chat later. I need to talk to Bethany."

He watched her go and smiled when the two women put their heads together and started giggling like teenagers.

He walked over to Sage where she was still standing with Ophelia. The two were engaged in a lively conversation about art. He wrapped his arm around Sage's shoulders and squeezed, grateful that he'd found her.

Ophelia looked at him and said, "You did good with this one, August. Your mom would be proud."

"She would." He smiled down at Sage as she leaned into him and wrapped her arms around him.

"I think mine would, too," Sage said, making August feel about ten feet tall.

"Okay, time for the tarot reading," Bethany called from her spot where she reigned in the parlor with Serena next to her. "Sage? August? It's your turn."

August groaned but didn't protest when Sage grabbed his hand and pulled him into the parlor. All of Sage's sisters were there, along with Serena and Ophelia. Talk about putting yourself on display. Tarot wasn't really August's thing, but it was Bethany's. So for Sage's sake, he'd endure.

"Okay, are we ready?" Bethany lit a candle and some incense and then started shuffling the cards. "Spirit guides, please tell us what's in the future for Sage and August."

She turned over a card and started cackling. "Oh dear. Well, this is a spicy reading, isn't it?"

Sage leaned over, reading the cards. Her face turned bright red, but she said nothing.

"Let me pull a few more just for clarity," Bethany said. After she flipped the cards, she raised her head and looked right at Sage and August. "Congratulations, you two. Looks like you found your perfect match. The cards say passion, intensity, and unity. This relationship is very sexual in nature and will continue to be throughout your lifetimes. But it's not just physical. It's emotional too. With both elements present, you'll find yourselves completely satisfied in more ways than one."

The room erupted with laughter, and Sage's face turned even redder. "Oh. Em. Gee. Did that just really happen? Did my grandmother really just tell me that I'm destined for great sex for the rest of my life?"

"She sure did," August said. "Can't say I'm unhappy about it either."

"Stop," she said with a laugh.

"Want to give these jesters a show?" he asked her.

Her eyes glinted with amusement as she nodded.

August didn't hesitate. He swept Sage up in his arms, bent her back, and gave her a kiss that left little to the imagination.

CHAPTER 28

LILY EASTON STOOD in the gallery, pretending to study the painting of Levi Kelley and Silas Ansell. It was on display as part of August's portrait series. It wasn't for sale of course. He'd given it to the subjects as an engagement present. But since this was August's gallery opening, they'd agreed to have it displayed to help garner interest in August's work. It was lovely and intimate, but ultimately, Lily believed it hadn't been needed. All of August's work had the same quality. There was no missing just how much of his heart he put into every piece.

She took a sip of wine and wondered when Braxton Kirkwood would move on. If he'd just go look at something else, she could slip past him without making eye contact. And she wouldn't have to see the disapproval in his eyes every time he looked at her.

"Lily!" Sage called as she hurried over to her and squeezed her arm. "You made it."

"Of course I did," she said to her older sister. "Where else would I be?"

Sage gave her a flat stare. "Behind your computer, working on—"

Lily quickly cut her off, knowing her sister was going to say her book. "I'm not the workaholic here," she said pointedly.

Sage threw her hands up and laughed. "Okay, point taken. I'm just glad you're here. Isn't it wonderful? I've already sold five of August's paintings. And two people tried to buy this one." She waved at Silas and Levi's portrait. "Can you imagine some rando having this hanging on their wall? It's just so..."

"Personal," Braxton said from behind them.

Lily swallowed an internal groan before turning around to face the owner of the outdoor sporting goods store. She'd met him at the Witches Ball a few months back and had enjoyed a night of dancing and flirting right up until she'd kissed him and then he'd bolted. Now every interaction with him was awkward as hell.

"Hey, Braxton," Sage said, squeezing his hand. "Thanks for coming. It's quite the turnout, isn't it?"

"It is. I should have hired you when we had the grand reopening for my store. We might have gotten more than two people just looking for a steal." He shook his head but winked, letting her know he was kidding.

Lily rolled her eyes. There was no store in town busier than The Enchanted Outdoors.

Braxton raised his eyebrows at her, and she mentally kicked herself. Obviously, he'd noticed her childish eyerolling. Why did this man always make her feel like she was doing something wrong?

"Problem?" he asked her.

Nope." She downed the rest of her wine and turned her attention back to her sister. "There's a piece over there I'm interested in." She pointed to the one that was of downtown, but it was sunrise and the streets were clear. No people. No cars. Just the town and the sunrise. It was her favorite time of day when she cleared her mind before diving into work.

"Oh, sorry, Lily," her sister said earnestly. "I didn't know you wanted that one. It's already sold."

"What? Already? Who bought it?"

"I did," Braxton said, raising his glass to her.

She carefully schooled her features, knowing that there was no way he could've known she wanted that painting, but for some reason her gut said he'd bought it just to mess with her. But why? "Congratulations." She glanced at Sage. "Excuse me. I'm just gonna go get another drink."

"Lily!" her sister called, but it was too late. Lily walked right past the open bar and headed outside to get some air. There was a light sea breeze off the bay, and off in the distance she thought she could hear the orcas talking to each other. It was just the kind of night she loved. If she didn't need to go back inside to support her sister, she'd just keep walking, let herself get lost in her thoughts, and then likely would end up at her computer, typing out the jumble of ideas that never seemed to stop coming.

"Why haven't you written about my store yet?" the familiar gruff voice of Braxton Kirkwood said from behind her.

She spun to look up into his serious expression. "You came out here to ask me why I haven't written about your store? Is that why you've been so..." She waved a hand at him. "Like this?"

"Yes, I came out here to ask you that. Did you think I didn't notice that you write about every single event in this town except when it comes to me and my store? Am I blackballed or something? And what the hell do you mean that I act like... 'this'? I don't know what 'this' means."

"I write satire, Braxton. Or did you miss that?" she argued, suddenly mad that he was attacking her for... what? Not including him in her weekly column? "I'm not a machine for promoting various businesses. I write what I think is funny. Like when Prim took her knitting on the paddleboard and I decided she was knitting the orcas sweaters. That's funny. Talking about fiberglass kayaks isn't really my forte. If you really want my attention, how about you work for it? Write to Endora and ask a question, or do something more interesting than buying up artwork before anyone else even has a chance to write a check."

"Interesting? You want interesting? Fine. Write about this." He grabbed her, pulled her into his arms, and then kissed her. Lily was stunned at first, not sure what to do, but then as his tongue tasted her lips, she opened for him and met him taste for taste and stroke for stroke, clutching his shoulders and wanting more—

He suddenly broke away and planted her on her feet. Then he cupped her cheek, looked her in the eyes, and said, "How's that for interesting?"

Before she could find her voice, he was gone.

DEANNA'S BOOK LIST

Witches of Keating Hollow:
Soul of the Witch
Heart of the Witch
Spirit of the Witch
Dreams of the Witch
Courage of the Witch
Love of the Witch
Power of the Witch
Essence of the Witch
Muse of the Witch
Vision of the Witch
Waking of the Witch
Honor of the Witch
Promise of the Witch
Return of the Witch
Fortune of the Witch

Witches of Keating Hollow: Happily Ever Afters
Gift of the Witch

Wisdom of the Witch

Witches of Befana Bay:
The Witch's Silver Lining
The Witch's Secret Love

Witches of Christmas Grove:
A Witch For Mr. Holiday
A Witch For Mr. Christmas
A Witch For Mr. Winter
A Witch For Mr. Mistletoe
A Witch For Mr. Frost

Premonition Pointe Novels:
Witching For Grace
Witching For Hope
Witching For Joy
Witching For Clarity
Witching For Moxie
Witching For Kismet

Miss Matched Midlife Dating Agency:
Star-crossed Witch
Honor-bound Witch
Outmatched Witch
Moonstruck Witch
Rainmaker Witch

Jade Calhoun Novels:
Haunted on Bourbon Street
Witches of Bourbon Street
Demons of Bourbon Street

Angels of Bourbon Street
Shadows of Bourbon Street
Incubus of Bourbon Street
Bewitched on Bourbon Street
Hexed on Bourbon Street
Dragons of Bourbon Street

Pyper Rayne Novels:
Spirits, Stilettos, and a Silver Bustier
Spirits, Rock Stars, and a Midnight Chocolate Bar
Spirits, Beignets, and a Bayou Biker Gang
Spirits, Diamonds, and a Drive-thru Daiquiri Stand
Spirits, Spells, and Wedding Bells

Ida May Chronicles:
Witched To Death
Witch, Please
Stop Your Witchin'

Crescent City Fae Novels:
Influential Magic
Irresistible Magic
Intoxicating Magic

Last Witch Standing:
Bewitched by Moonlight
Soulless at Sunset
Bloodlust By Midnight
Bitten At Daybreak

Witch Island Brides:
The Wolf's New Year Bride

The Vampire's Last Dance
The Warlock's Enchanted Kiss
The Shifter's First Bite

Destiny Novels:
Defining Destiny
Accepting Fate

Wolves of the Rising Sun:
Jace
Aiden
Luc
Craved
Silas
Darien
Wren

Black Bear Outlaws:
Cyrus
Chase
Cole

Bayou Springs Alien Mail Order Brides:
Zeke
Gunn
Echo

ABOUT THE AUTHOR

New York Times and USA Today bestselling author, Deanna Chase, is a native Californian, transplanted to the slower paced lifestyle of southeastern Louisiana. When she isn't writing, she is often goofing off with her husband in New Orleans or playing with her two shih tzu dogs. For more information and updates on newest releases visit her website at deannachase.com.